M000219496

WHAT DID TED HAVE?

A NOVEL

JOHN J. CARROLL

Copyright © 2019 John J. Carroll
All rights reserved
First Edition

NEWMAN SPRINGS PUBLISHING
320 Broad Street
Red Bank, NJ 07701

First originally published by Newman Springs Publishing 2019

ISBN 978-1-64531-402-8 (Paperback)
ISBN 978-1-64531-403-5 (Digital)

Printed in the United States of America

ACKNOWLEDGMENTS

WHAT DID TED HAVE? COULD not have been completed without the extraordinary secretarial assistance provided to the author by Elaine Carroll, Aemilia Ferreira, and Christy Daniels.

CHAPTER 1

BEFORE DAWN ON THE SATURDAY morning of September 16, 1944, a convoy of twelve 1938 Chevy buses painted olive drab and carrying the distinctive markings of the United States Army rumbled slowly out of Fort Devens in the tiny Massachusetts town of Ayer just thirty miles west of Boston. The few citizens of Ayer who saw or heard them early that late summer morning knew with some certainty that each bus contained new recruits who had just finished four days of indoctrination at Devens, and were heading south, probably to Fort Dix in New Jersey, for basic training before being shipped overseas to Europe or to the South Pacific to help close out the war.

Pvts. Robert Mohegan and Manny Lopes pushed down the crowded aisle of bus number four to try to find seats together. Because their surnames began with the letters *L* and *M*, they had been called out together at least four times during the last three days. Each time, they anxiously waited in various lines to be handed their new army gear. Waiting gave all the recruits time to chat with each other.

Robert almost immediately sensed that Manny was the type of guy who could figure out what was going on during the chaotic entry process as the men were shifted from room to room and building to building. At each stop, they were examined from head to toe, had their blood drawn ten times it seemed, given all kinds of forms to fill out, and listened to hardened officers with ribbons on their chests and stripes on their sleeves give them instructions and ideas about what their lives might be like for the next few years. For Robert, who had just finished an easy summer working for fifty cents an hour at the Boston Edison Company on C Street in South Boston after graduating in May from South Boston High, the process was jarring. He had never experienced anything like that.

Manny seemed to not be bothered so much; he seemed to always anticipate the next irritation, which made it easier for both of them. Manny Lopes began and ended each conversation with "amigo" or "amiga," depending on the gender of the person to whom he was talking, because, to him, everyone *was* a friend. His easygoing personality came from his father who left Mexico in 1930 for Southern California to work in the vineyards of Napa Valley. Manny was seven then. He worked in the fields alongside his father for twelve years. When the war began and the wine industry began to falter, his father decided to move east to Massachusetts to join the thousands of migrants in the defense industry. It was relatively easy then to become an American citizen, so the whole Lopes family had done so. They rented a third-story apartment in Everett, a working class city just north of Boston. Manny's father, a naturally gifted auto mechanic, easily found work in the General Electric plant in nearby Lynn, assembling turbo chargers for Allied planes. There Manny was drafted into the army. He had just turned nineteen. With his jet-black hair, deep brown face, sparkling white teeth, and brawny build, he could easily have been a high school Lothario, except that Manny had never seen the inside of a high school. Besides, Manny's inborn nature, he was uncommonly wise, gentle, and highly moral, making any young guy or pretty girl in his inner circle of acquaintances to instantly trust him and want to become his friend.

So it had been with Bobby Mohegan. Their few hectic days together at Devens made him feel like he and Manny played in the same sandbox as toddlers. Bobby Mohegan—Bobby Mo to his friends beyond his family circle—was the son of John and Mary Mohegan who, like many young Irish men and women, left the "old sod" to seek prosperity in the U.S. Soon after World War I, hundreds and thousands of others like them had emigrated in the last century, fleeing the Great Famine that had caused a million deaths in Ireland in the mid-1800s. Most of the survivors headed to America, mostly to New York and Boston.

The Mohegans settled in South Boston, a section of Boston northeast of the city proper, which was heavily populated by Irish Catholic immigrants. John Mohegan, who knew no trade, soon found work as a gravedigger in the local cemetery. His younger brother Jim and his wife Helen followed suit. Anomalously, both men—who were still in their thirties—shifted from playing Irish football and hurling to watching American baseball. They quickly become enamored with the local team, the Boston Red Sox. The brothers, as was the custom of Irishmen in those days, waited until they were in their midthirties to get married. Jim and Helen never had children. John and Mary had two at a time when families of ten were common. In Bobby's father, John's case, he and Mary also had a daughter, Elizabeth, who had given signs from her childhood that she would be a Roman Catholic nun.

Robert Mohegan (Bobby Mo) had been inducted soon after he graduated from South Boston High in May 1944 at eighteen. By then, he was tall and skinny with reddish brown hair, blue eyes, and a modicum of freckles on a thin and bony face. He was a happy kid growing up with no plans for the future beyond high school, except maybe to play for the Red Sox. Bobby Mo loved the Red Sox hated the New York Yankees. There was this other plan he had stored away in his mind. He wanted to marry Marie Callahan who lived just two streets away and have a lot of kids. Never leave Southie! In actuality, his dream of hitting a grand slam to win the seventh game of a World Series for the Boston Red Sox was dashed when he failed to make the varsity baseball team at Southie High. But there was always Marie. She had flaming red hair; blue eyes; and a tall, well-proportioned body. She and Bobby had been in school together since first grade. By senior year, they were a twosome. Bobby made sure of that.

As they boarded their bus, Manny politely offered Robert the window seat, but Robert has chosen the aisle so "my long legs can swing out into the aisle as much as possible."

Manny smiled and asked, "How long's the ride, any idea?"

"Six to eight hours, I think," guessed Bobby Mo, "with a lunch and a leak break. What was that crap we had for breakfast? Was that scrambled eggs? I change my mind. Ten hours. We're crawling already even with no traffic."

Summer in New England in September of 1944 had not yet surrendered. It was going to be a warm and humid day. Each window on the bus had been slid back as far as possible to catch the occasional breeze, but it was not going to be a comfortable ride. They tried not to talk, trying to shut his eyes to gain back missing sleep. It didn't work. The anticipation of what lay ahead for them was too high.

Manny turned from watching rural wartime New England face another day of a long-drawn-out war to ask, "Bobby Mo…"— by now, he knew Robert Mohegan preferred to be called Bobby or Bobby Mo—"Bobby, can I ask you something? Kind of personal, do you mind?"

The question got Bobby Mo's attention. "What kind of question? We don't know each other that well, Manny."

"No, we don't. It's not about you personally though, it's about your family." Manny's dark brown face lit up in a broad smile of assurance. He had black eyes that almost squeezed shut when he did, his white teeth shining. He touched Bobby Mo's arm lightly and pulled it back. He asked, "Bobby, did something real bad happen to you? Like someone in your family get killed?"

"How did you know?"

"You talk in your sleep. A couple of times when you were in that bunk next to me back in Devens, I heard you kind of mumbling something about your dad in the middle of the night. You were sobbing." Again, he touched Bobby's arm.

"I don't want to talk about it, Manny. I really don't. Do you mind?"

"No, of course. I'm sorry I brought it up."

They reached Boston now for sure. People were heading for work. Traffic was light but increasing. Not many cars were on the roads, none newer than 1940 models. There were no new cars being made in America. Buses, trolleys, transit systems, bicycles, and their own legs carried most people to their wartime jobs. An hour later, they were on U.S. Route 1, the old Boston Post Road, heading toward New York and New Jersey.

Bobby Mo nudged Manny. "I'll tell you the story."

"You don't have to, Bobby. I'm sorry I brought it up."

"I know I don't have to. I want to. My dad loved baseball. You like baseball, Manny?"

"I don't know much about it. We played soccer back in Mexico. Some guys played it though, *Béisbol!*"

"Soccer?" Bobby displayed a fake disgusted look. "That's such a stupid game. No one ever scores."

"You asked me."

"You're right, I did. Anyway, my dad loved baseball. You have to understand this, Manny. He came over from Ireland. You ever meet anyone from Ireland, Manny?" Manny shrugged. "Anyway, my father's name was John Mohegan. He was tall, taller than me, and I'm six feet."

"Was?"

"Was, Manny. Somehow when he came here during the first war—1918 or so—he and his brother Jim both took to baseball like fish to water. You talk kind of funny, Manny. You know that? So my father and his brother, my uncle, they talked with what they called a *brogue*."

"A what?"

"A brogue. The Irish people talk with an accent. They say 'ye' instead of 'you.' Never mind! Anyway, they both loved baseball and the Red Sox."

"That's the Boston team?"

"Yes. On Sunday afternoons, Dad and me, we would take the trolley and bus from Southie, that's South Boston where we lived. I told you about Southie, right? So we'd meet Uncle Jim at the games. They played at a stadium called Fenway Park. It's old, built in 1912."

"Yeah, you told me about South Boston the other day."

"Well, anyway, three years ago in 1941, it was just about this time in September 14, I remember the date, the Sox were playing terrible. They were way behind the Yankees."

"The Yankees? You're a Yankee, right?"

"I'm a Yankee all right, but not a New York Yankee. They're the best team in baseball. Anyway, the game ends. The Sox lost as usual.

There were only about 3,000 people in the ballpark that holds about 35,000. The season is almost over. At fifteen, I'm walking along with my dad and uncle Jim. Not much of a crowd, like I said. I'm happy enough munching on an ice cream bar. A ways from the ballpark, the crowd thinned down when this guy came toward us. He knew we've just left the game He looks at my dad and says, 'What did Ted have?' So my dad says, 'What did Ted have? I don't get it, Bobby.' Ted Williams was a young baseball player, Manny, was famous after two years. The guy is asking how Ted played that day. So my Dad says, 'Two for four.' My uncle says, 'Two for five.' The both of them begin arguing right there on the street. I'm not about to listen to them argue so I say, 'Look, I kept score on my game program but I tossed it in that wastebasket back there.' I decide to go back and get it. It's sitting right on top of the pile. I look and begin to say, 'Ted had—' *Bang!* And I hear a shot. Manny, I'd never heard a shot before but I knew it was one. It came from some distance away. People stopped, someone screamed, and everyone up ahead seemed to be yelling and running. As I ran toward them, the crowd tightened into a little knot. I push through. Everyone is in shock or in a panic or crying. Manny, my dad was sitting there on the cement sidewalk. He fell against the legs of some guy. He's looking at me, Manny, but not really looking at me. He's dead. My dad is dead, Manny! I could see why when I got close to him. He'd been shot between the eyes, Manny."

Overwhelmed with his story, Bobby Mo began to sob softly. This time, when Manny placed his hand on Bobby Mo's arm, it stayed there.

"Oh my god, Bobby! My *amigo*…oh my god!"

Bobby couldn't continue. The buses continued to rumble toward New York. It was midmorning by the time they reached Hartford. The recruits were fully awake now. They stopped once at a Howard Johnson's. Refreshed, they began to talk and the bus filled with chatter as the convoy approached New York.

Bobby Mo wanted to finish the story of his father's death. "My dad was only fifty-nine. My mother, she's from Ireland, too, is still alive. She's sixty or so. I have a sister who's only fifteen. She says she wants to be a Catholic nun. A religious sister, Manny. You understand?"

"Yeah, I know. *La relegiosa.*"

"Everyone in Southie had a hard time with it, Manny. Marie too. She still has a hard time thinking about it."

"Marie?"

"Oh yeah, Marie's my girlfriend. I met her in high school. We were in love, at least I was. She said she loved me. I think we'll get married as soon as I get out."

"Married? Bobby, you're only eighteen. How old is Marie, sixteen?"

"Same age as me."

Feeling that Bobby Mo needed to talk more about his father's death, Manny spoke up. "But, Bobby, what happened right after... you know, when your father got shot?"

"Well, of course I went crazy. Crying and kissing my daddy, telling him he wasn't dead. It was horrible. I don't personally remember much of what happened next. But here's what I was told later. A few minutes after Dad was shot, a cop—a Boston cop—came running up all excited and out of breath. He pushed his way through the crowd. He began to yell, '*Oh my god! Oh my god!* I had hoped the shot went wild, but it didn't.' He told anyone who would listen that he was walking on Jersey Street away from the ballpark when he saw a young guy trying the handles of parked cards. The kid finally found one unlocked and tried to open the passenger door. The cop came up behind the kid and grabbed him. I didn't hear this myself, I heard it later. The kid, who was a big guy, wrestled with the cop, spun away, and somehow pulled the cop's gun out of his holster. It was a Colt .38 revolver, I later found out. He stepped back, holding the gun with two trembling hands, according to the cop. Then he said, 'Get away! Don't come toward me or I'll shoot!' The cop said he had no intention of arresting the kid. It was Sunday afternoon for God's sake! The kid was probably hungry, looking for food. But the cop must have looked like he was going to move forward because the kid pulled the trigger. *Bang!* They both looked at each other in shock. The kid dropped the gun, turned, and ran. The cop had no choice, he watched him go. Then he heard the yelling. He ran toward the crowd, hoping for the best. He got the worst."

"My god, Bobby! Did they ever find the killer?"

"Nah. They searched for him that night and a couple of days after but they couldn't find him. There was some news about it in the papers and the radio, but not much. I often wonder where he is. At first I wanted to kill him if they found him, but not now. I would like to see him get caught though. It was a great strain on my mom, my little sister, and me. It still is. I think of my dad every day. He was such a good father, a good guy. I loved him. I wish I could meet the guy face-to-face to let him know what he did to me and my family.

Manny held back his tears; Bobby could not. No more words of any consequence passed between them for the rest of the trip.

CHAPTER 2

Fifty miles away from the slowly moving convoy in a small sweltering office in barracks 124B in Fort Dix, Sgt. Andrew Vitkus was waiting with heart-pounding anticipation to meet the young recruit he just realized might be the son or a relative of the man he shot and killed in Boston three years ago. That realization came to him an hour earlier as he casually thumbed through the list of recruits he would help train for the next few months. There it was! Robert Mohegan, Boston. Mohegan was a name he never wanted to see again. Each day for the last three years, his thoughts had mercilessly taken him back to that awful day.

That September Sunday started out all right. He woke up near noon from a fitful sleep in the tiny house trailer he shared with his father in Pawtucket's Riverside Park. He had no plans for the day except to have a beer or two with his buddies from high school and play a little flag football and maybe shoot a little pool. His father was already sitting at the kitchen table drinking a Schlitz, in a filthy mood. Andrew wanted no part of his old man that morning. He decided to skip his shower and shave and get out of there as soon as he could. But the old man was looking for a fight.

"No church today? No Mass? Your mother always wanted you to go to Mass. Remember how she took you every Sunday?"

"And you remember that Ma is dead? You remember, Dad, why she died and how she died, Dad? Now you don't have that beautiful redhead as a wife anymore and I don't have a mother."

Andrew knew he shouldn't have reminded his father that his wife had gone out on foot looking in different beer joints for her husband one cold night eighteen months ago. She had been found raped and murdered in a parking lot the next morning. No matter that the guy had been caught and was awaiting trial. Had Charlie Vitkus not been out drinking that night, Andrew's mother would still be here. The old man, his face flushed, started to get up from the table to put his hands on his boy when the only door in their house flew open.

"Hey, what's going on?" It was Tommy "Fat Boy" Vitkus, Andrew's wannabe Capo half brother. Tommy was a carryover from one of his father's past relationships.

"The little asshole here is at it again, Tommy. Bringing up his mother's death."

By this time, Andrew was up and getting dressed. He knew Tommy would quickly join ranks with his father. He wanted no part of what would most certainly be a wasted argument. "I'm outta here."

He pulled on his Pawtucket High School track sweatshirt, rushed past Tommy, and stumbled down the two loose wooden stairs. And outta there he went. Andrew did not play stickball that day or pool. Instead, he decided to hitchhike up to Boston for no good reason. An hour later, as he stood by the side of the road looking for a ride to Boston, Andrew began to think about how he had just treated his father.

He remembered as a kid how the old man used to take him on short trips when his routes were local. They always had great times together. Charlie Vitkus worked gigs delivering jewelry manufactured in and around Pawtucket to stores in Downtown Boston. Sometimes he would be gone all week, making deliveries to places as far west as Chicago. Then he would find a mom-and-pop motor court by the side of the road, park the big truck, and look for a place to eat and toss down a few cold ones. A few beers often led him to more and many women. By the time Andrew was in high school, his father was an alcoholic whose poor driving record and unreliable work habits caused him to be blackballed by the jewelry industry in Pawtucket. Andrew kicked at a couple of early fallen leaves and vowed to try to improve the relationship when he came home that night.

Two rides and two and a half hours later, he was in Boston. It should have been only one ride but he had to tell the first guy to stop the car in Attleboro and let him out or he'd beat him up. The second guy was on his way to Boston to see the Red Sox play the Yankees so Andrew got dropped off near Fenway Park.

Now with the new recruits just hours away, the memories of what happened next came crashing down on Sergeant Vitkus again. His heart began to beat rapidly.

He had been hungry when he set foot in Boston. He wouldn't take anything from the first guy and the second one apologized for not having anything to offer him. Andrew hadn't taken any money with him in his haste to leave the trailer.

Jersey Street, which housed the grandstand entrance to the old ball-park still had a few people and cops wandering around as the vendors got ready for the exiting crowd. He walked away from the ballpark until he came to the nearest residential area of apartment houses. There were cars parked here and there. Andrew's mother instilled in him what God said about not lying or stealing. Andrew had no problem with that. But on that afternoon, the hunger had gotten the best of him. He couldn't see anyone on the street so he began to look into parked cars in hopes of seeing some food. In the front seat of a beautiful 1939 DeSoto coupe, he spotted a half-eaten sandwich with a wrapper. The window was partway down. He reached in, but his fingers could only touch it. He couldn't grab the thing. He needed to open the big door but it was locked. He began to pull on the handle. A heavy hand suddenly slapped his right shoulder.

"All right, kid, that's it!" Even before he turned to face the stranger, Andrew could see his reflection in the window. It was a cop! He spun instinctively and in a panic tried to push him away with both hands. "Hey, kid! Take it easy! I'm only—" Andrew pushed harder. The burly policeman didn't like to be pushed around by a skinny kid.

Sitting uncomfortably in that tiny office, Sergeant Vitkus remembered exactly what happened next.

"Son, take it easy or I'll have to arrest you!" Their two bodies came together. Suddenly, Andrew felt his hand on the cop's gun. He pulled it easily out of its holster. The cop stepped back. Andrew's back was against the DeSoto. "Hey, kid, watch out! That thing's loaded!"

"Get away or I'll shoot! Get away!" His two hands gripped the big revolver, still trembling. "Get away!"

Suddenly, the big gun fired. The shock for the two men was profound. They looked at each other in astonishment. Now the cop was angry.

"You, young bastard! Give me that thing!"

As he stepped forward, Andrew ducked under his wild swing. Then he threw the gun onto the tiny lawn of a nearby apartment building and started running. He ran faster than he ever had on the Pawtucket High track team. He could hear the cop yelling for help. But there was no one within earshot.

A knock on his office door snapped him out of his unpleasant memories.

"Yes?"

The door opened and a young corporal leaned in, "Sarge, I'm told the convoy has entered the grounds. They should be here in fifteen minutes."

Andrew glanced at the list of names of the 180 recruits again, looking for one in particular. He was hoping that he misread it the first time. He did not. *Pvt. Robert P. Mohegan, Boston, Massachusetts.* Boston was big, there are probably a lot of Mohegans there.

As he randomly ran away that Sunday, the sound of the gunshot was still in his ears. In a few minutes, he came to what looked to him like a swampy area with shoulder-high grass covering it and paths leading into its banks. Only a long time later did he learn that it was called the Fens, an urban marshland that was part of Olmstead's famous Emerald Necklace. But on that day, it was a place to hide and rest until he could figure out what to do next.

Seated in the high grass, he began to rationalize. He only fired one shot so the chances were one in a zillion that it actually hit anyone or anything. It probably landed somewhere, lost forever. Not even the cops would care. He settled in on a soft spot. "I'll sleep here tonight," he told himself, "then head back home tomorrow morning." He knew then he couldn't live with his father any longer. He was about to be drafted anyway so he would sign up for the army or marines as soon as possible. Maybe America wouldn't even get into the war in Europe. Maybe he would never even get shot at or even get a chance to kill a Nazi or a Jap. He pulled off his sweatshirt to use as a pillow and had begun to doze off in the high grass that late summer afternoon when he heard muffled voices. Could the cops be looking for him? No, those people were coming from the game. Two or three guys. He listened as they walked by twenty feet away.

"Cripes! I can't believe it."

"Me neither. We come to see the Sox play the Yankees and a guy gets murdered almost in front of our eyes. Shot in the head. I can't wait to tell the wife when I get home. I hear it was a young kid who fired the shot."

The voices faded away. Andrew began to tremble in his hiding place as the cool afternoon turned to dusk. Suddenly he became aware of flashing blue lights, soft sirens, and lots of voices in the distance and then nearby. They were looking for him. That cop must have reached a call box and reported what happened. His one-in-a-zillion shot must have hit someone. He scrambled from his spot and plunged deeper into the high grass. He came to a small, slow-moving stream and stumbled alongside it until he reached a small arched stone bridge. He looked deep into the darkness under it and decided to take a chance. He crawled along the bank and found a spot where he could perch precariously in a half-sitting position. He thought no one could see him there even if they shined a flashlight.

As night came, the lights reflecting in the muddy water began to fade. So did the voices. He dozed off occasionally, almost falling from his perch into the muddy water. It was only two feet deep. Eventually, he heard nothing but all kinds of eerie night calls. He shivered all night and hardly slept. A couple of rats scampered by. He was terrified.

"Sarge, they're here. They'll need you in a couple of minutes." It was the impatient corporal again.

"Okay, corporal. I'll be right there."

His thoughts still pulled him back to that day. He remembered how he had stumbled out of his hiding place into a beautiful late summer dawn.

His dungarees and sneakers were muddy and wet. He made an effort to wash off the muck. Then he began walking with no sense of direction. Now he was really hungry. He thought of finding a cop and turning himself in but he saw none. If he had, he probably wouldn't anyway. He noticed that he was in a town called Brookline. Up ahead, he saw a tractor and a box trailer in front of a small mom-and-pop store. It was open early. The driver was leaving the store with his coffee. He was about to pull himself up into his cab when he saw Andrew.

"Well, look at you. Bad night there, buddy? You look hungry. Need a cuppa coffee and some doughnuts?"

"Yes, sir. I'm starved."

"Where are you headed? You live here in Brookline? You don't look like you do. This is a rich town, you don't look rich. My name is John. What's yours? I'm heading for New Jersey, place called Fort Dix. Stuff in the box is for the army. Uniforms, mostly. Made up in Lowell.

"I live in Pawtucket."

"Good. You want a ride with me? I go right by there. I'd like company. Don't worry, I'm married with kids."

"Yes, sir. But first, could you buy me the morning paper? The Boston Post right there. I…I want to see how the Sox did yesterday."

"Sure will. Here you are."

Settled in the cab munching doughnuts and sipping coffee, Andrew looked with trepidation at the front page. There it was, below the fold:

Man Killed at Red Sox Game
Shot outside Fenway Park

> *John T. Mohegan, 59, of South Boston was shot on Jersey Street and killed yesterday afternoon as he was leaving the Red Sox game with the Yankees.*
>
> *It is believed that Mr. Mohegan did not know his assailant, who, up to late Sunday night, had not been found or identified.*
>
> *Police Commissioner James O'Toole said that all of his force was on the lookout for the killer who was described only as a tall, young white man wearing a white shirt and dungarees.*
>
> *Crap! No mention of the sweatshirt. He had left it behind.*

"Sarge. They're here. You ready?

"Yeah, line them up. I'm coming."

Sgt. Andrew Vitkus, the killer of John Mohegan three years ago, was about to meet a new soldier with a surname he never wanted to see or hear again.

CHAPTER 3

OVERNIGHT, THE POUNDING OF A severe thunderstorm and heavy rain on the roof of their barracks had kept most of the recruits from sleeping soundly. But it also had chopped the temperature and humidity. Everyone felt better.

Even though their bunks were not close, Bobby Mo and Manny easily found each other at the mess hall. The cool weather, strong coffee, and hot cereal had refreshed all the recruits.

"You OK, Manny?"

"Yeah. G'morning, Bobby."

"Coffee's good. Hot."

"Bobby, what did you think of what happened last night?"

"Last night? Oh, the storm, I didn't mind it much. I—"

"No, Bobby, I mean when we all got off the bus. The sergeant, what was his name? Begins with a *V*…"

"Yeah, he tried to scare us with all that talk about what we were going to go through the next coupla months. I kind of expected it. No big deal."

"No, Bobby. No. Didn't you see what he did? The roll call?"

"Whaddya mean, the roll call? I kind of expected it."

"Bobby Mo," said Manny as he leaned forward across the table to make himself heard above the chatter of hundreds of nervous recruits trying to get to know each other. "Bobby Mo, listen to me. We're all standing there, hot as hell. Can't wait to take a shower and hit the sack. And then, Bobby, what happens? The sergeant introduces the company captain who says a few words and takes off."

"So? He didn't have much to say."

"Bobby. I know. But the sergeant what's-his-name says to the corporal, 'Call the roll.' You remember? And the Corporal says, 'But, sergeant, it's pretty late and there are a lot of guys. Maybe we should wait until tomorrow morning—' 'Call the roll,' he says. This time, we could all tell he meant it. *Wow!* The way he snapped those words off, 'CALL THE ROLL!'"

"Yeah, I remember, Manny. I could tell he was ticked off about something. So what?"

"Bobby Mo, listen to me. The corporal starts off with the *A*s and *B*s like he should and then the Sergeant gets exasperated. You could tell. He says to the corporal, 'Hurry it up a bit, corporal. You're going too slow.' Then the corporal gets pissed, he speeds it up. When he gets to your name and what happens…?"

"Everyone laughed," said Bobby Mo.

"Why? Because when the corporal calls out, 'Private Robert Mohegan,' you say 'Hee-yah" instead of 'here'," Manny said, emphasizing the *R* by rolling it deliberately so Bobby Mo will understand again that he speaks with a strong Boston accent.

"Yeah, Manny. So what? I know I speak funny, so do you. What's your point?"

"Here's my point, P-r-i-v-a-t-e Mohegan. Here's my point. What happened next?" said Manny. Without waiting for an answer he continued, "The poor corporal, he's calling the names out damn fast by then. He only gets to the *P*s—Paulini or something like that—and the sergeant says, 'That's it, corporal!' 'Sir?' the corporal says. 'I'm only—' Then the Sergeant says really firmly, 'That's it, corporal. It's late and it's hot. These boys need a shower and some rest. See you all at 8:00 a.m. on the parade grounds. Good night.' That was a strange way of ending it, don't you think, Bobby? I mean, when he got up around your name, he cut it off…the calling of the roll, I mean."

"He went past my name, Manny. A few names past."

Manny sighed. "Yeah, I suppose, Bobby. I suppose. You all done? C'mon, Bobby, we've got to get to the parade grounds…wherever they are."

*****

Sergeant Vitkus had been up since 0530 hours. He had already run three miles and done his aerobics just as he did every morning. He hadn't slept well. The combination of the storm and how he acted the previous evening kept him from sleeping well. He wondered if any of the recruits had noticed his strange behavior. Probably none. They were tired and ready for bed anyway. He cursed himself for letting his emotions unravel in front of the corporal. As soon as he could, he would apologize to him personally. He wasn't even sure of the corporal's name. Lucky for him, the company commander had left the scene. Otherwise, he would have been reamed out for the way he treated the corporal.

But now he knew who Pvt. Robert Mohegan was and that he was from Boston. That *hee-yah* last night nailed that down. He began to wonder again what, if any, relation the kid was to John Mohegan. He knew he had to find out.

But first, standing before the ragtag group of recruits on the parade grounds, he reintroduced himself. "Good morning, gentlemen. At ease. That means you can relax for a couple of minutes. Let me introduce myself again. My name is Sgt. Andrew Vitkus. Me and the company commander, the Corporal over there, and I are going to make combat-ready soldiers out of you in two months. I know a lot of you guys think the war is about over and ya probably won't see any action. Maybe so. But just in case it's not, we want you to be ready to kill a lot of Nazis and Japs and try to keep you from getting killed so you can get home to your mothers and make love to all those girlfriends waiting for you back home. You ever heard the term 'asses and elbows'? Probably not. In the army, we use it all the time. Look around you. All over these parade grounds, there's cigarette butts and gum wrappers. Every single one has gotta be picked up every day. So get going. Now! All I want to see for the next thirty minutes is asses and elbows. Get going!"

Where was Private Mohegan? Which one was he? Sergeant Vitkus wanted to get a good look at the kid whose father or uncle he may have murdered. As the recruits streamed past him to perform their first official act of public service, Sergeant Vitkus tried to pick out Robert Mohegan again. Most of the men avoided his eyes. But one in particular seemed to stare right at him, a heavyset Spanish kid. Dark skin, that wasn't Mohegan. *Oh, there is Mohegan, right behind the Spanish kid.* Skinny, tall, narrow face, prominent nose, reddish hair or what was left of it after the scalping back at Devens. Sergeant Vitkus knew he would eventually have to talk to the kid without appearing to have any special interest in him. But for today and a bunch of tomorrows, it would be all business. Mohegan needed to be made combat ready like the rest of these young men whose lives had been entrusted to him for a very short time.

CHAPTER 4

ON THE FIFTH DAY, AFTER a breakfast of eggs, bacon, sausages, ham, and pancakes loaded with syrup, Bobby Mo told Manny that he thought basic training wasn't going to be all that bad. "After all, all we've done so far is go on a few short runs, learn how to march—left, right, left, right—make our beds, listen to a few talks about the army from some sergeants and lieutenants and stuff, and eat. The food's good, don't you think, Manny?"

"It is, Bobby Mo. By the way, have you noticed that after that first day, Sergeant Vitkus—Is that how you say his name?—has disappeared? We haven't seen him at all. He was supposed to be our drill sergeant. All we've had are substitutes who don't seem to give a crap."

Two more days passed and suddenly at 0530 hours, the occupants of barracks 124B were startled by the distinctively hoarse voice of Sergeant Vitkus. "OK, boys. Up and at 'em! I expect to see all of you on the parade grounds at 0800. You've got ninety minutes to shave, shower, and eat! Then you know what's next. Those grounds look pretty bad since I've been gone. Asses and elbows! Let's go!"

Somehow his voice felt reassuring. Sergeant V's substitutes just didn't have his commanding persona. This day proved to be grueling. They had to run over, under, and through an obstacle course that left all of them tired and sweaty. Some of the guys who were way out of shape couldn't finish.

"Manny," Bobby Mo said as soon as they had finished and were gulping down lots of water under the shade of a maple tree, "did you notice how the sergeant talked to the guys who were having trouble?"

"Nope, I didn't, Bobby."

"He was really nice to them. Actually, he put an arm around one guy's shoulders—that fat kid over there—and seemed to be reassuring him. I noticed though that he reamed out a couple of guys who were clearly screwing off."

"I think I knew why he was gone, Bobby. I heard a couple of corporals talking. His old man was sick so they let him go home for a few days."

"*Wow!* Did he die?"

"I don't think so. But I think he has cancer."

That night at dinner, Bobby Mo nudged Manny, "Hey, you see that guy over there? The red-haired guy?" Now he was talking to the several other recruits at the table as well. "That guy is nuts. He's whacked out."

"Why? What do you mean? Who is he? Where's he from?"

"He's from Arkansas, I think. His names is…Richard Chesterfield. That's what you smoke, isn't it, Manny? Chesterfields?"

"Be quiet, Bobby." Manny is always polite. He would never say *shut up*. "What's wrong with him?"

Everyone at the table was looking at Bobby Mo now. He explained, "His bed is next to mine. He talks out loud all the time, says he hopes Hitler wins the war. Hates authority. Does not like Sergeant Vitkus at all. Says so all the time. And one other thing, he says he doesn't need the shooting range. He knocks off squirrels from two hundred feet in the Ozarks with a .22 carbine."

"Bobby, did you tell Sergeant Vitkus about him?"

"No," Bobby said loudly so all the table could hear, but he looked right at Manny and mouthed, "And you know why."

Manny decided to keep an eye on the kid from the Ozarks. As often as possible, he would sidle up to him to listen to what he was saying. Most of it was sheer nonsense but there certainly was a theme to everything he said. Mostly it was how he wanted the war to be over so he could go home to his momma and daddy. He cursed every word from Sergeant Vitkus' mouth. Private Chesterfield, in Private Lopes' opinion, was clearly wacko. How did he even get past that psych exam back at Devens?

Manny, like all the new soldiers, was a bit intimidated by their drill sergeant. But he finally got up the courage to speak to him. At a break in the middle of a three-mile run on a warm day in late September, he wiped the sweat off his face, gulped the last of the water from his canteen, and walked over to Sergeant Vitkus. "Sarge, could I speak to you for a second?"

"Sure. How's your buddy from Boston. What's his name, Mohegan? You guys seem to hang close. What's the problem...uh, what's your name again?"

"Lopes, sir. Manuel, Manny Lopes." As quickly and as clearly as he could, Manny tried to explain that Private Chesterfield might eventually mean trouble for the whole company, particularly for the sergeant himself.

"Uh, I know the kid. He does seem a bit nutty but I don't think he'll be any trouble. And I'll be sure to watch my back." Then in that commanding voice of his, Sergeant Vitkus let the tired recruits know that a shower and dinner were only a mile and half away. "Let's go, let's go! Up and at 'em! Lopes, you there, take the lead with me. You're a pretty good runner, Lopes. High school?"

"Nope, Sarge. Didn't get that far. How about you?"

"Pawtucket High School track team. I was pretty good."

In spite of the fact that he had seemingly brushed off Manny's warning as he ran alongside him, Vitkus began to wonder about Private Chesterfield.

"The kids is nuts!" he said to himself. "I'd better watch him closely. I better try to talk to him directly." Then he nodded to Manny who was having no trouble with the last leg. "How's Mohegan doing? You two seem pretty close. Did you know each other before?"

"Nope, Sarge. We met at Devens. Good guy. I liked him soon as we met. His story is pretty sad though. It kinda weighs him down."

"Whaddaya mean?" Sergeant Vitkus visibly lost his breath for a couple of steps. He knew what Manny was about to tell him. He didn't want to hear it. He had hoped that Private Mohegan was only a nephew, as if that would have reduce the enormity of what he had done.

"Yeah, Sarge, Bobby—by the way, he likes to be called Bobby Mo. He's at a Red Sox game three or four years ago, I don't remember exactly when, when his dad gets shot and killed right in front of him. It was a random shot supposedly from some kid a few hundred yards away who got caught by a cop as he was breaking into cars. He grabbed the cop's gun and fired a shot. He got away, they never found him—You OK, Sarge? You look a bit out of breath."

"I'm fine. Just tripped on a pothole back there." Sergeant Vitkus didn't talk out loud much the rest of the way in. But he did talk to himself mentally. *I wasn't trying to break into cars, just that one DeSoto. Only to grab that sandwich I was so damn hungry. I wonder what it was. Turkey? Ham? And I didn't mean to shoot that guy, it just went off. Damn it! Why? Why did I do that?*

CHAPTER 5

THE DAYS AND WEEKS PASSED quickly. By early November, the New Jersey weather had turned cold and raw. Manny and Bobby Mo began to expand their circle of friends, although they managed a few minutes together every day.

Sergeant Vitkus seemed to be paying no special attention to Private Mohegan but he actually couldn't get him out of his thoughts. He wanted desperately to confess to him but every time he thought about it, he would think about the possible consequences and he would back off. He also hadn't found time to privately talk with Private Chesterfield who seemed to have calmed down or at least wasn't drawing any undue attention to himself.

There were hardly any radios available to the recruits and none of them had time to read a newspaper if one became available. Most heard from loved ones and friends back home, so word got passed around the barracks about how the war was going in both theaters. It seemed to be going real good in Europe, not so good in the Pacific. But it was clear that the Allies were winning. A kid in the barracks from Brooklyn whose nascent bookmaking career was interrupted by the draft, was taking wagers on the exact day the war would end. Most guys were betting part of their monthly pay of $460 that it would end in January in Europe and May or June in the Pacific. All the talk gave rise throughout the whole camp to the rumor that the troops in Europe would finish off the Nazis. The troops at Fort Dix would be shipped off, so the rumor had it, to one of the Pacific islands to await the invasion of Japan in May or June. Those expectations, as unreasonable as they turned out to be in hindsight, led to the thought that since they wouldn't be shipped out right away, some lucky ones might be able to score three-day passes for the Thanksgiving holiday only a month away…and then at Christmas, who knew.

Bobby Mo wrote nearly every day to Marie, less often to his mother and sister. He also stood in line three or four times a week to call Marie collect from the only payphone in the Post Exchange (PX). She responded to his letters once a week. "I'm not really a good letter writer," she wrote back one time when he complained. She answered his phone calls with a friendly but never passionate tone. "Yes, I care for you. You know I care for you," she would respond when he got whiny with her.

He began to wonder if some "draft dodger" at the Edison had taken his place in her affections or one of the jocks from high school, but most of them would be somewhere in the armed services by now. Once on the phone, he mentioned it, trying to sound as if he were joking. She sternly rebuked him. Still…

*****

By now, recruits were going to the shooting range nearly every day. They had been taught by Sergeant Vitkus everything there was to know about their M1 carbines. From each three-mile trip to the range at the edge of camp, they became good shooters. They had learned on the first trip out that there were three official levels of marksmanship: marksman, sharpshooter, and expert. The word got out quickly among the smart-asses that it was okay to be ranked as a marksman or sharpshooter. But if you were really good and got ranked as an expert, you might soon find yourself in New Guinea or Papua or some other godforsaken battleground in the Pacific, aiming your M1 at some poor Jap's head. But then again, maybe one of those Japs would have you in his sights the next day. So everyone from Sergeant Vitkus' Barracks, no matter how good he could shoot, managed not to become an expert. Everyone, that is, except Private Chesterfield. He was boastful about reaching the expert stage.

In mid-November, the recruits jumped down from the 4×4 that brought them to the range for one last cold and raw morning of shooting. Manny sought out Bobby Mo.

"Bobby Mo, you see Chesterfield today?"

"No, why?"

"He's acting really strange. He didn't get a pass for Thanksgiving so he's pissed. He says only the sergeant's favorites got them and he looked straight at me when he said it. He knows you got one too. He knows we're pals. He says he hopes the Nazis win the war, he doesn't want to go fight them."

"What's he say about the Japs?"

"I don't think he knows who they are."

"Are you kidding?"

"Yeah, but all he talks about is how he wishes the Germans would win the war. And boy, does he hate Sergeant Vitkus! *Wow!* Bobby, you're near him on the firing line, aren't you? My station is about twenty-five spots away from him. Bobby, please, please keep an eye on him when we're firing. I'm going over to let the sergeant know that I'm worried."

Fifty recruits took their stations and waited prostrate on the cold ground for a now familiar voice to give them the go-ahead to begin firing. That voice came booming over several loudspeakers stationed up and down the line. Each word of the command was spoken slowly with precision. "Ready on the right? Ready on the left? Ready on the firing line? The flag is up. The flag is waving. The flag is down. Commence firing!"

Almost as soon as Bobby Mo's finger squeezed the trigger, he became immersed in what he was doing. After all, this was going to be a free day of shooting, no checking on scores today, and he was trying to score big. Each man's ear muffs made the cacophony caused by fifty M1s firing almost simultaneously an almost distant sound. Behind the men on the line, their commanding officer and a couple of drill sergeants strode back and forth, providing assistance whenever it was needed. One of them, of course, was Sergeant Vitkus. Occasionally, a man would raise his hand asking for help in unjamming his rifle or looking for some other assistance. He would push himself up to a squatting or kneeling position while one of the senior officers helped him. Other than that, the firing continued routinely.

Then twenty minutes into the shooting, Bobby Mo lost concentration on the target when his peripheral vision caught an unusual movement to his right. Private Chesterfield was rising to his feet twenty feet away. Before Bobby Mo could even react, Chesterfield was on his feet. Bobby quickly ripped off his ear muffs as a tidal wave of sound from thousands of gunshots washed over him. He put down his weapon and scrambled to his feet. Chesterfield already stepped out of his assigned space and was walking down the aisle behind all the prostrate shooters toward Sergeant Vitkus who was squatting down beside a soldier who signaled for help. With his back toward Chesterfield, the sergeant didn't know his life was in danger. Chesterfield carefully aimed at his easy target from thirty feet, then he moved closer. The recruit the sergeant was helping looked up and stared incredulously at the M1 aimed in his direction.

Private Chesterfield was screaming but no one could hear him. But the stream of invectives, heard only by him, caused seconds to pass before his finger would squeeze the trigger. When he did fire, for the first time during all those trips to the Range, Private Chesterfield missed his target. Bobby Mo had scrambled to his feet and with all of the ferocity a former junior varsity football player could muster, had hit Chesterfield with his right shoulder at the back of his knees. The one .30 carbine cartridge fired from Private Chesterfield's M-1 did not enter the back or head of its intended target—Sergeant Vitkus. Instead it flew off into the ether at a thousand feet a second. Chesterfield went down hard, face-first, his M-1 bouncing a few feet away from him, with Bobby Mo hugging his legs at first, then trying to get on top of his thrashing body to keep him down.

Soldiers nearby began to sense something happening behind them. They quickly put their own weapons aside, scrambled to their feet, and ran to help subdue the raving and incoherent soldier who was reaching vainly for his M1. No military police (MP) were nearby. It took some ingenuity with bootlaces and belts for his fellow soldiers to bring a thoroughly exhausted Private Chesterfield under control. Word passed quickly up and down the line, "Some guy has gone nuts!" Gradually, even before they heard the command from the loudspeakers, "Cease firing! Cease firing!" The now curious men on the line began to put down their weapons to look toward the bizarre scene.

Sergeant Vitkus had been absorbed in helping the soldier with the jammed magazine so he was one of the last ones to realize what was going on. He hardly knew how to react when he finally scrambled to his feet and saw the crowd surrounding Private Chesterfield. He knew about the private's bizarre behavior, of course. Just this morning, one of the other recruits, Lopes, warned him to watch out for Chesterfield. "Damn it!" he swore almost out loud as he hurried over to where Chesterfield sat bound and gagged, eyes bulging at the sight of his nemesis. *I should have paid more attention to what Lopes had been telling me*, he thought. He tried to take control of the situation and the crowd milling around their "prisoner." "Look, guys, everything will be OK. We'll get the MPs over here right away. Private Chesterfield will be evaluated. He just had a bit of a breakdown. He'll be OK."

But one of the recruits suddenly spoke up to him, "Sarge, you don't understand. He was tryin' to kill *you*. I saw it all. I happened to look up and I saw him aiming his weapon right at you from ten feet away before Mohegan knocked him down."

The recruit the sergeant was helping spoke up, "Sarge, it's true. I saw that gun pointed right at me and you. He was going to shoot you and maybe me. Then Mohegan—I think it was him, I couldn't see that much—knocked him down."

"Sergeant, those men are right on! I saw it all!"

All eyes turned in the direction of the loud voice. Every man in uniform, with the one exception of Private Chesterfield, snapped to attention and saluted. There on the grassy bank behind the firing line and on the soldier's side of the four-foot high chain-link fence that bordered the range stood, unmistakably, a brigadier general. Sergeant Vitkus recognized him immediately as the base commander, Gen. Avery McDonald. No one else knew the general's identity.

General McDonald walked slowly down the bank to where the crowd gathered. He talked in a loud enough voice so he could be heard by everyone. "*Whew!* I'm a little out of breath from climbing over the fence. My adjutant, Col. Ashby Williams, and I were driving around the base and decided to stop for a few minutes to watch you fellows shoot. Then we saw this soldier"—he pointed to the now involuntarily mute and bound Private Chesterfield—"get up and walk in your direction, Sergeant...?"

"Sergeant Vitkus, sir."

"Right, we saw his weapon pointed right at your back, Sergeant Vitkus. My god, we were transfixed! There was nothing we could do from my Jeep behind the fence. Then we saw this other young man get up. Where is he?"

Someone in the crowd nudged Bobby Mo and whispered, "Raise your hand."

Bobby hesitated and then said, "I think it was me, sir."

"That's right, it was you. What's the matter with your right arm? What's your name?"

"I hurt it when I tackled him, sir. He kind of fell on it. Pvt. Robert Mohegan, sir."

"Sergeant,"—the general was now looking directly at Sergeant Vitkus—"this young soldier here saved your life. He actually saved your life. I saw it with my own eyes. There's some irony there, sergeant. I mean, here you are teaching all these boys how they can survive in a battle somewhere overseas and here's one who saves your life right here in Fort Dix. This young man has got to get some sort of commendation, don't you think, sergeant?"

"Yes, sir, general. Yes, sir."

Sergeant Vitkus walked the general back to his Jeep through an opening in the fence a hundred feet away. *Ironic indeed*, thought Sgt. Andrew Vitkus as the MPs came to take Private Chesterfield away. He announced the end of the day's shooting exercise. Before he left, the sergeant called Manny Lopes over. "I'm going to leave a note for you and Mohegan. I'll put it in your mailbox tonight. Be sure you get it in the morning OK?

"OK, sir. I'll make sure."

CHAPTER 6

A SENSE OF EUPHORIA SWEPT OVER all the troops as they gathered their gear and piled into the 4x4s that would take them back to their barracks. Although they hadn't been officially told yet, they knew that the afternoon, as cold and raw as it was shaping up to be, would be their own. In just two months as soldiers, they had learned the meaning of SNAFU. They instinctively knew there would be no plan in place to account for how they would spend the rest of the day. On the trucks, the men who were close to the action tried as best they could to explain what happened to those who were far away from it. Private Mohegan was the center of attention on his truck, getting slaps on the back and congratulations from everyone around him.

Although they were on separate trucks on the ride back to camp, Bobby Mo and Manny were excited about what Sergeant V's note might say. Manny told Bobby Mo about it as they trudged toward their separate trucks. Manny Lopes' and most of the troops, whose shooting exercise in the morning had been cut short, had a chance that afternoon to catch up on their reading or letter writing and to grab a couple of beers at the PX. No one else knew of the warnings Manny gave to the sergeant about Chesterfield and he wasn't about to tell anyone.

There was no cushy afternoon for Bobby Mo. He was summoned to central command to be interrogated about what happened by a captain and a couple of lieutenants on the record. First, they congratulated him on his lifesaving actions then they asked him to explain what happened as best he could. A secretary took it all down. He felt important, but he kept telling himself not to make Sergeant Vitkus look bad for not listening to several warnings about Chesterfield that he and Manny—especially Manny—had given the sergeant.

"Did Private Chesterfield have it in for Sergeant Vitkus?"

"Have it in? I don't understand, sir."

"Was he angry, as far as you know, about anything the sergeant said to him or did to him?"

"I don't know, sir. Maybe so. But I don't know of anything. I did know this. He was mad at the whole world. He was always saying things like he wanted the Nazis to win the war so he could go home. I think the sergeant overheard him a couple of times and told him to knock it off. 'This is a great country. You could be court-martialed for talking like that.' Chesterfield—Private Chesterfield probably didn't like that very much."

"Where is he from?"

"Arkansas, I think. The Ozarks, wherever they are. He was a great shot, by the way."

"So, Private Mohegan, how did you happen to notice Private Chesterfield's actions?"

They listened to Bobby Mo's account for quite a while, asked him a few more easy questions, and dismissed him with more plaudits and handshakes. On his way out, Bobby passed a few of his bunkmates in the outer office. They were there to give their sides of the story. Bobby tried to act as if he wasn't a hero, but he knew from the looks on their faces that they thought he was.

CHAPTER 7

THE TWO OF THEM COULD hardly wait to read the sergeant's note. They found it in Manny's mail slot. When he opened it, there was no salutation and no name at the bottom. It was also written in large capital letters.

THE TWO OF YOU SHOULD COME TO THE
NCO CLUB AT 1800 HOURS TOMORROW NIGHT.
JUST GIVE YOUR NAMES TO THE GUY AT THE
DOOR.
DO NOT MENTION THIS TO ANYONE.

The noncommissioned officers club, *wow!* The possibility of a good meal and a few drinks with some of the camp's *hoi polloi* started them laughing and smiling to the extent that some of their buddies began to question them pointedly at breakfast.

"You two engaged or something?"

"Bobby Mo, you gonna get a medal?"

"Something's going on between you two."

"Nothin'," Bobby Mo said to all of the good-natured jibes.

It all faded away eventually. That day passed quickly. Everywhere he went, Bobby Mo was the center of attention. Chesterfield made no friends in the barracks so when the incident at the shooting range was spread, he was only referred to as that "nutty guy" or "screwball" or worse.

Bobby Mo snuck away early from scraping the paint off the poorly painted windows on his barracks. He laid on his bunk and fell asleep until Manny nudged him. "Bobby, wake up. We gotta get dressed. It's five."

"Oh yeah. Manny, what do we wear? Our class Bs?"

"Yeah, if we wear our class As, we'll look like we're gonna be in a parade or something and we can't go in these rags."

They both laughed at Manny's inference that their almost new fatigues were "below them." They pretended not to hear or notice the wise-ass boos and shouts thrown their way as the rest of the guys headed for the mess hall and they were headed for the NCO club. But they were smiling broadly as they walked up the street. The NCO club was brightly lit so they had no trouble spotting Sergeant Vitkus with a couple of his buddies at his table. After formal introductions were made all around and a pretty waitress brought a pitcher of foamy beer and menus to the table, a sergeant name Rick something or other looked at Bobby Mo, nodded toward Sergeant Vitkus, and asked Bobby, "So you're the guy who saved this asshole's life?"

Bobby Mo quickly answered, "I guess so, sir."

The ice was quickly broken after Sergeant Rick said, "What part of my question are you agreeing with, the first or the last?"

In itself, ordering from a menu was a treat. Bobby Mo and Manny had to be encouraged to choose what they wanted and eat as much as they wanted. So they did. The conversation ranged from how the war was going to how ridiculous it was that the St. Louis Cardinals and the St. Louis Browns played in a wartime World Series. Manny had no idea what they were talking about.

CHAPTER 8

AT FIRST, THE THREE OF them fiddled with their utensils and sipped empty coffee cups. Sergeant Vitkus finally push his chair back a little and turned to Bobby. He could hardly stand the fact that his heart was beating so loudly. *Couldn't they hear it?*

"*Uh*, is it OK to call you Bob or Bobby or Robert...?"

"Bobby, sir."

"He likes to be called Bobby Mo, Sarge."

"Oh, Bobby Mo. *Wow!* OK. So Bobby Mo, I hardly had a chance to thank you for what you did. I guess you saved my life. I didn't even know what was going on as my back was turned. I still can't figure out why Private Chesterfield"—he was careful to use no derogatory nickname in referring to his assailant—"was angry at me."

Bobby Mo tried to clear it up. "He was angry at everyone, Sarge. He wanted the Nazis to win. He talked all the time about going home to the Ozarks. I guess you kind of stood in his way. Otherwise, I don't have any idea why he wanted to shoot you. I do know one thing. If he actually wanted to shoot at you, he wouldn't have missed." They all laughed.

Sergeant Vitkus flicked the ash from his cigarette into his coffee cup and asked, "So where are you from Manny, or should I call you Manuel?" He didn't care that much about what Manny would tell him, but he didn't want to press Bobby Mo immediately.

"Manny, Sarge, I'm from a place just north of Boston. It's called Everett. My family came up here two years ago from Southern California so my father could get work in the defense industry. He found a job in an aircraft engine plant in Lynn. That's a little north of Boston also."

"So that's *North* Boston?"

Both men laughed at that. "There's no such place as North Boston!"

"Oh!" Andrew felt tightness in his throat. He could hardly continue. "West Boston?"

"No, Sarge. All that's left is South Boston. That's where I'm from, Sarge. South Boston!"

Bobby Mo grinned at the way he thought he and Manny had confused the sergeant. They hadn't. Sergeant Vitkus wanted desperately to hear from Bobby Mo's lips that Manny Lopes had somehow gotten the story all wrong, that it wasn't *this* Bobby Mohegan whose father he killed. Maybe *this* Bobby Mohegan was a nephew of John Mohegan who lived in another part of Boston. Maybe he was not a Mohegan from South Boston but from some other part of the city and that he was not related to the late John Mohegan from South Boston. He managed a weak smile. "Well, we all knew you're from Boston, Bobby. How do you say 'here" again?"

"Hee-yah, Sarge. Hee-yah." Now Bobby Mo asked a question, "You ever been to Boston? Ever been to Southie?"

Sergeant Vitkus knew he had to couch his answers carefully or else the two young men, especially the perceptive one, Manny, might ask more questions and somehow get him to say too much. "Southie? No. Boston maybe once, a long time ago." They all laughed.

Sergeant Vitkus didn't want to talk anymore. He started to rise up from his chair, but Manny, emboldened by the sudden somewhat intimate nature of the conversation, began to pry further.

"So if you don't mind, Sarge, where are you from?

"Pawtucket."

"How long you been in? We heard you've been in three years and you already saw some action."

Sergeant Vitkus sat back down. "Yeah, I joined up straight out of high school three years ago in October 1941. We weren't even in the war then. I was deployed overseas to the Pacific in July 1942, Guadalcanal. Then I got sick. Real sick with dysentery. They couldn't cure me there so they put me on a deadhead flight back here. I'm OK now. I think you guys can attest to that."

He had to explain to Bobby Mo and Manny about Guadalcanal. Bobby Mo was tired. He wanted to get some sleep after yesterday's excitement. But Manny wanted to know more about their Sergeant.

"So, Sarge, if you don't mind, how'd you get promoted so quickly? I mean, if you don't mind my asking. *Wow*, in just three years!"

"I was lucky. Had a couple of open shots at two Japs, helped capture a couple more. They made me a sergeant. Then I got sick, like I said. Now I'm ready to go back soon. How about you, guys?"

"We're not so sure, are we, Bobby?" said Manny. Bobby was nodding off. He didn't care much about the sergeant's life history. "*Erm*, that sounds like you're telling us something, sarge," said the always perceptive Manny.

"Maybe. By the way. And you better keep your mouths shut, the two of you. I'm gonna get a chance to recommend that a couple of guys in our company be promoted to corporal." He paused before adding, "You both put in for passes for Thanksgiving, right?"

"Yes, Sarge," they both answered. "We got 'em."

"How about you, Sarge?" Now Manny was really trying to know this man better, this man who had worked so hard to turn them into soldiers. "You going up to Pawtucket?"

"I may. I hope so. My father isn't feeling well."

"We kind of heard, Sarge. Rumors travel fast."

"Well, anyway, if it all works out, I may be able to get you two a ride. Maybe all the way to Boston with another sergeant, and maybe me. Don't let anyone else know."

"We won't, Sarge." This time, it was Bobby Mo who answered. He was happy at the thought of seeing Marie again and, of course, his mother and sister.

*****

On the Monday before Thanksgiving, both Bobby Mo and Manny found a note in their respective mail slots.

BE AT GATE 10 ON WED AT 0600 HOURS.
I WILL BE THERE.

Listening to the talk among their fellow soldiers that week, they figured out that most of those with passes were being picked up by relatives. Some were hitching rides. Some were taking buses from the temporary bus terminal right in the middle of the camp grounds.

They'd have to get up at 0400 hours to shower, shave, get dressed, and packed to get to gate 10 by 0600 hours since it was half a mile away from their barracks. They agreed the hustle would be worth the effort. They made it to the gate a little out of breath by 0545 hours. No sign of the sergeant. The sun wouldn't rise until 6:30. It was still dark and cold. They sat on a low stone wall. Several vehicles went in and out, showing their identification to the lone MP on duty. Still there was no sign of sergeant Vitkus or his friend. They began to worry a little. There was nothing to do but talk.

Bobby Mo, despite their three-month-old relationship had not learned much about Manny's family, decided it was time to ask. "Manny, I don't think I know…I should have asked you before. You got siblings? How old's your mom and dad?"

"Two brothers. Twins, fifteen years old, still in high school at Lynn English High. Fernando and Frederico. My mom stays at home. You've heard me say before that my dad worked at the GE plant in Lynn near where I live. I think they make engines for our planes. I don't know much more. My mom does people's laundry to help out. Here, I've got their pictures in my wallet. Can you see? It's dark. There's Mom and Dad and Nando and Rico. Good kids."

The sun had risen when at 0700 hours, a big black 1938 Buick Special stopped momentarily at the gate, flicked its headlights, blinding Bobby Mo and Manny, and screeched to a halt in front of them.

Sergeant Vitkus didn't even bother to get out. He leaned out the passenger side and shouted, "Good morning, boys! C'mon, the trunk's open. Throw your stuff in there. Get in the back. Glad you made it on time. I did say 0700 hours, right?"

"Yes, Sarge. That's what you said, Sarge."

Inside on comfortable seats at the back, Bobby Mo and Manny didn't have a chance to get their bearings before the big Buick made a quick U-turn, slowed a bit passing the guard shack, and then hit the highway for points north.

Sarge turned to them. "This here's Sgt. Rick O'Brien. You met him the other night. He's gonna take us all the way. Rick lives in Southern New Hampshire, don't you, Rick? That's like South Boston, right, Bobby Mo?" Then he twisted all the way around to reach over the back of his seat and handed them two hot coffees and a bagful of warm doughnuts. "While you boys were still sleeping, me and Rick here did our two-mile run and had ourselves a little off-campus breakfast. It was tough to find a place open at 5:00 a.m., but we finally did a couple-a miles away. Sorry we were late. I hope the coffee makes up for it."

"Sure does, Sarge," they answered.

With Rick's heavy foot on the gas, Sergeant Vitkus guessed they'd be in Boston in the early afternoon. For two hours, the conversation was of a desultory nature. Weather, not bad for Thanksgiving week. War could be over in Germany by Christmas. Sports, the Cardinals beat the Browns in the St Louis Trolley Car World Series. No one cared much. Eventually, things grew quiet. Each to his own thoughts.

Sergeant Andrew Vitkus had a lot to think about. He thought about his father. Andrew hadn't been home a lot since he exploded out of the trailer that fateful day to head to Boston. At each visit, he and his father made efforts to be civil. It worked all right, mostly because Andrew made sure he didn't stay in the trailer much. He managed to hang out with one or two of his high school buddies who escaped the draft. The girls he hung around with in high school were already married or were working somewhere in the defense industry. He vowed not only to mend the relationship with his father for good, but also to talk to him about his illness. Charlie Vitkus had lost a lot of weight. Although he was once a big man, he now was thin and looked haggard. The one short visit a few weeks ago scared Andrew. He vowed to himself to see what he could do while he was home to help his father.

In Guadalcanal, before he got so sick, he shot and killed more than the two he had told the boys about at the NCO club. Then there was the grenade he tossed right into the Japanese machine gun nest. He would never know anything about those men or their families. But Bobby Mo's father was different. He didn't know John Mohegan, but he certainly knew Robert Mohegan. And he knew one day he would have to confess about the killing to Bobby Mo first and then, he guessed, to the cops. He desperately wanted to share his anguish with someone, maybe his father. The old man was sensible when he was sober. As he did nearly every day for the past three years, he ran through a gamut of haunting scenarios if he were to confess.

- *I'm a killer. Let's face the facts, I am a murderer.*
- *But it was accidental. Totally accidental.*
- *I'm not really a murderer.*
- *Maybe I should confess. What good would that do? Who would benefit? How is it possible that this kid in the backseat who just saved my life is the son of the guy I killed? Am I ever going to confess so this "thing" won't drive me mad? Am I going to end up like Chesterfield? How am I going to end this hypocrisy with Bobby Mo? What will happen if I confess? Will I be demoted? Will I be discharged? Will I be tried and convicted of murder?*

To each question he asked himself, he gave himself varying answers each time. Sometimes he ended up in the brig or in front of an army firing squad. Sometimes he got off scot-free and lived happily ever after. As they approached Connecticut, he forcefully stopped daydreaming and broke the silence in the car. "Say, Bobby Mo, you got a girlfriend, don't you? Up in South Boston?"

Bobby snapped out of his own reverie. "Yeah, Sarge, I do. I think I told you. Her name is Marie, Marie Callahan. She's a redhead. Beautiful."

Manny, who was looking out the window for a restaurant where they could eat lunch, spoke up without ever turning his head. "Sarge, I keep telling Bobby that she's not ever going to marry him. She's nineteen and he's only eighteen. She is beautiful though. I've seen her picture. He has it in his wallet."

Sarge swung all the way around to face Bobby Mo. "Is she that pretty, Bobby? Let me see her picture."

"*Aw*, Sarge, I don't really want to dig it out now," he sniffed. "I'm almost nineteen."

"Let me see it. That's an order, Private Mohegan." They all laughed. Bobby pulled the photo out of his wallet and handed it to Sarge. "It's black and white but I got it colorized. Her hair is redder than that."

Sarge reached back and grabbed the photo. "She *is* really pretty, Bobby." Then for some reason, his heart seemed to skip a beat. He stared at the worn headshot longer than he should have. "*Wow!* She really is pretty. I'll tell you why. She looks just like my mom. Her hair is a different style but it's red. So was Mom's. She's gorgeous. I'm going to keep the photo, OK, Bobby Mo?"

"*Aw*, c'mon, Sarge. Give it back please!"

Sergeant Vitkus handed the photo back to Bobby, but for some reason he was reluctant to do so. He wanted to look at Marie again. She looked so much like his mother.

Manny dared ask the obvious question, "*Wow*, Sarge, is your mom still alive?"

"No, she died in an accident."

No one dared to ask the obvious next question, "What kind of accident?" If they had, they somehow knew, they wouldn't have received an answer.

As Bobby Mo was inserting "Marie" back in his wallet, he suddenly gushed to no one in particular. "Marie is really a good girl. I don't have to wonder if she'll run off with some other guy. One time she told me that the first man to touch her breasts will be her husband on their wedding night. She's Catholic. She goes to Mass every day on her way to work." Bobby Mo's *naïveté* momentarily stunned the two men up front. Not so Manny. He had heard his friend talk endlessly about Marie. He admired Bobby Mo for speaking that way about the girl he loved. Bobby Mo slumped back in the seat when he realized from the silence and the side glances up front that it might be wise not to talk about Marie for a while. Ove the shoulders of the two sergeants, he pointed ahead, "Hey, look! Pawtucket, Rhode Island, fifty-six miles. You're almost home, Sarge!"

Sarge had been thinking for a while about where he would be dropped off when they got close to the trailer park. He directed them to an intersection a quarter of a mile away. "Here," he said. "Drop me off here. I live around the corner."

"You've got a lot of baggage. I can—"

"No, here is fine, Rick. It'll be easier for you guys to get out of the city and back on route 1. But before we go, let's swap telephone numbers. Where are you guys gonna meet on Sunday morning? It should be at no later than 0800 hours. I have a friend in Boston. I might go up there Saturday and stay with him overnight. So you might see me there on Sunday morning."

Each of them scribbled telephone numbers on scraps of paper and passed them around. Manny suggested a meeting place "at the corner of Boston Commons."

"Boston *Common*," interjected Bobby Mo. "There's no *S* in Common."

"On Tremont Street, just below the State House. There's a subway stop right there," continued Manny.

"We'll meet there at 0800 hours. Eight o'clock," Sergeant Vitkus added.

"Yeah that's right 8:00 a.m.!" they all shouted, glad to be free for a few days from Army time.

*****

As he slowly trudged the half mile to his trailer in Riverside Park, Sergeant Vitkus knew why he hadn't let them pull up at his door. As he walked along, his heavy duffel bag shifted from one shoulder to the other. He knew it wasn't so much about being embarrassed about where he lived, but more about the possibility of his father greeting them at the door drunk. He had no friend in Boston. He hoped that Marie would be there to see Bobby Mo off on Sunday morning so he could meet her. As he walked, he muttered out loud

44

to the empty streets, "Here I am thinking about the girlfriend of the guy who saved my life a couple of days ago. Worse, I'm the guy who killed his father. It was all so crazy. I'll bet Marie has fat legs and a big butt." He tried not to think about her untouched breasts.

The two wood steps were still wobbly. He turned the knob and opened the door.

CHAPTER 9

H E EMBRACED HIS FATHER PERFUNCTORILY. Andrew did all he could do to keep from recoiling from the shock of touching his father's gaunt frame.

"Any plans for Thanksgiving, Dad?"

"Naw, not much. I haven't had time to buy a turkey."

"Why don't I buy one, Dad. Then you and me and Tommy can have Thanksgiving together. Maybe some of your buddies can come too. You're a good cook. You used to help Mom with the meals a lot."

"I miss her."

"I know you do, Dad. Me too. By the way, one of the guys I rode with showed me a picture of his girlfriend. She looked so much like Mom, it scared me. Gorgeous too. This kid is only eighteen. He saved my life on the shooting range a couple of days ago when this whacked-out recruit tried to shoot me in the back. I'll tell you about it later."

Andrew spent part of the late afternoon on the eve of Thanksgiving at Rigotelli's market, buying a fourteen-pound turkey with all the fixings. He brought it all home to his father who was making an effort to remember how to prepare a Thanksgiving dinner. It all came back as he worked. He made a few phone calls and got a promise from some of his former drinking buddies that they would be there.

"Three o'clock sharp! Tommy said he'd come too. Nowhere else to go anyway."

*****

46

Up in South Boston, Bobby Mo got left off by Sergeant Rick at the bottom of C Street. He ran up the hill lugging his duffle bag. He was out of breath when he knocked on the door. It was thrown open almost instantly as he plunged himself into his mother's welcoming arms. He hadn't seen her in months. Already her small flat had that turkey-roasting-in-the-oven smell.

"Where's Sis?"

"She'll be home in an hour or so, don't worry about her. First, tell me about what life is like in the army. I know you'll want to see Marie sooner than later." They sat on his favorite couch and reminisced about the one who wouldn't be with them for the fourth year in a row. He asked her if she had heard anything about the killer from the police department. "Nothing. Not a thing," she said. Her Irish temper rose a bit at the thought. "I call them all the time, I don't think they care. Glory be to God, Bobby, I miss your father so much. I ask the Blessed Virgin every day when I pray the rosary that he'll get out of purgatory and into heaven as soon as possible." Her eyes twinkled as she continued, "He wasn't a perfect man, as ye and I well know." They both laughed and remembered the times when big John Mohegan would come home after he "had a bit of the drink taken." She continued, "I also will tell ye that I pray to the Virgin every day that they'll catch the guy who did it. I'll give him a piece of my mind, I'll tell ye that." She sniffled and added, "If I live that long."

"You will, Mom. They'll catch him, Mom. I'm sure they will. And I'll do the same thing. I wonder whoever or wherever he is, if he even thinks about it anymore. It was just a random shot. Maybe he doesn't even know he hit Dad."

*****

Sergeant Rick apologized to Manny about not being familiar with Boston's winding street system. Manny was no help, he couldn't explain to the sergeant how to get from Downtown Boston to Everett. So with an apology and a promise that he'd get a map to find their meeting place on Sunday, Manny was dropped off at a subway stop where he hailed a cab and made his way to Everett with a few bucks in his pocket. He ran up the three flights as fast as he could. Inside, they all heard the sound of his boots on the stairs so the door was already open when he reached for it. Hugs and kisses swallowed him up.

CHAPTER 10

THANKSGIVING DINNER WENT SURPRISINGLY WELL in the little trailer. Five members of AA, including Charlie Vitkus, one grey-haired lady named Mae who appeared to be the girlfriend of Mel, one of Charlie's old drinking buddies, plus Tommy and Andrew all sat on worn-out kitchen chairs and boxes around a small rickety table loaded with a surprisingly good turkey dinner. Tommy complained about the lack of booze but he got no sympathy from the rest of them. Afterward, three or four of the guests remained to watch game shows on a blurry twelve-inch television set. The war caused the traditional football game between the Detroit Lions and the Green Bay Packers to be canceled.

"I read somewhere that someday these pictures are gonna be in color," said Mae. She was greeted by silence. "None of you guys can read anyway." she snorted.

Finally by eight o'clock, the dishes were done and put away and the guests were gone. Only the three of them remained: Andrew, his father, and Tommy. When Andrew realized that Tommy was nodding off on the only sofa in the trailer, he purposely kept the conversation with his father low and on mundane subjects until he was sure his half brother was asleep. He knew if he spent some time on the subject of his father's sobriety, Tommy would have no interest in the conversation. When he saw that his tactic to knock out Tommy was beginning to work on his father, he spoke up.

"Dad, there's something I need to talk to you about."

Charlie Vikus thought he knew what was coming, a nice talk about how Andrew was proud of him now that he was on the wagon for the umpteenth time coupled with a mild lecture on how he could stay on it this time for good. He got the talk, but it was less about alcohol than about his health. Had he gone to the doctor or the hospital about his weight loss? He had. What did they say? They're running all kinds of tests. He'll be all right. Then Charlie turned the tables and began to ask questions of the son he had hardly seen since he had joined the army almost three years ago. What happened in the Pacific? Was Andrew going to get a medal for the Japs he had killed on Guada—What? How did he get so sick? Was he going to have to go back? When did he think the war would end?

Andrew realized that his father was now fully alert and engaged in the conversation. An hour had gone by. He glanced over at the sofa. Fat Boy looked like he was deep in sleep. "Dad, I have something serious to talk to you about and it's not about you. It's about me."

At first, Charlie didn't grasp that his son was going to share a piece of his life that no man before had ever accessed. "You're getting married? Who is she?"

"No, Dad! Now shut up and listen. This is important." Andrew started to talk. Words wouldn't come out at first. Then he buried his face in his hands and began to cry. When he looked up, he wiped at his tears with his forearm. "I killed a man, Dad! I killed a man!"

"I know you did, son. But this is war."

"Dad, this was three years ago. Before the army, before the war. You remember the time you and I went at it and I ran out and I didn't come home until the next day?" And so for the next hour, Andrew told his story to his astonished father who began to cry with his son. "Dad, Mom always talked to me about God and I believed her. Now I'm not sure. Dad, tell me, if God is so good and so all-powerful, tell me why he allowed all that to happen. Why did I decide to go up to Boston? Why did I pick that car? How did that cop see me when I looked around and there was no one there? Why did that gun go off? Why did that damn bullet hit that guy, John Mohegan? Why didn't he turn his head this way or that or walk slower or faster so the bullet would miss him?"

"I don't know, son. I sure don't know."

"And tell me this, Dad, tell me why the son of the man I killed is in the group of recruits that I'm training. Tell me that." And then he had to explain all over again what happened on the shooting range. "The kid saved my life. Now he trusts me and somehow we're friends. I think we're gonna be good friends. I can't tell him I killed his father, I cannot do it. Dad, help me!"

For two hours, Charlie Vitkus explored options with his distraught son hoping to offer him advice that might begin to heal his tortured soul. In the end, when they both were exhausted from the most emotional conversation they had ever engaged in, Charlie offered his son only one piece of advice. "I'm not sure what will happen if you confess, son. But I do know this. You have to confess. At least to—What's his name?—Bobby Mo and maybe to the authorities. You'll never have any peace until you do."

"What's my dear brother have to confess?" Over on the couch, Tommy was yawning and stretching.

"What did you hear, Tommy?" demanded a shocked Andrew.

"Nothing. Just the last part about you needing to confess something. Has my big brother been naughty with the native girls on the islands?"

Andrew wasn't sure he could believe Fat Boy but there was nothing he could do about his concerns. He figured there was nothing Tommy could do with his newfound knowledge even if he heard the entire conversation so he let it go. Andrew slept late on Friday. In the afternoon, he borrowed some tools from his father and repaired the two loose steps. Then he cleaned up around the trailer, both outside and in. He felt better by the end of the day. He felt even better as the relationship with his dad was slowly beginning to be restored.

Yesterday's conversation about John Mohegan picked up where it left off. This time, Fat Boy wasn't around. "You're gonna have to confess sometime, Andrew. The sooner, the better."

Andrew knew the old man was right, but he also knew he couldn't face up to confessing to Bobby Mo or to anyone else for that matter...at least not right now. He also knew for sure that he'd never have peace until he did. Somehow he managed to function in the three years since the killing. At times other thoughts would push

John Mohegan aside for a while. It happened on Friday while he worked on the stairs. He just couldn't get the redhead up in Boston who looked so much like his mother out of his mind. He told himself that if he could just see her or talk to her briefly, he'd be all right. He knew his only chance—and even that wasn't guaranteed—to meet her before he went overseas again was for him to be part of the group getting together on Sunday morning in Downtown Boston because she'd probably drop Bobby Mo off. But that meeting place was for-ty-five miles away and in the wrong direction. How would he get there so early in the morning? Hitching a ride at 5:00 a.m. was fool-ish as no cars would be on the road. Any car on the road at that time would be driven by drunks.

Then he thought of Tommy. He had a car of sorts, a 1940 Plymouth, as Andrew remembered it. He's gonna want his gas paid for, back and forth, and more. He couldn't be trusted, of course, so Andrew could not tell him too much about the last two months. He reluctantly made the call. Tommy agreed and mysteriously told Andrew that he was flush, a big hit at the track, and there would be no *quid pro quo*.

*****

Up in South Boston, Bobby Mo was getting itchy and his mother knew it.

"Robert, it's time ye called Marie. It's time ye go see her. She's probably anxious. Ye can see your sister early tomorrow, before din-ner. By the way, your uncle Jim is coming by tomorrow for dinner. He…he's been very helpful to me since his brother died. He's been around a lot."

"MOM! Is Uncle Jim trying to flirt with you?"

"No, it's nothing like that, son. He knows I'm lonely."

"And he's lonely too, Mom!"

"Call Marie. By the way, before you run off, I'd appreciate your company at the seven o'clock Mass in the two days ye are here."

*****

The sun was setting over Downtown Boston as Bobby Mo ran to Marie's house on A Street two blocks away. Big Mike Callahan greeted him with a bear hug.

"She'll be right down, Bobby. She's been waiting for ye all day. How long are ye home for? Here's Marie now."

She was luscious in a sleeveless, jeweled-neck white frock that complemented her bright red hair and blue eyes. "You'll have to excuse my hair, Bobby. I just showered and didn't have time to dry it. We're going for a walk, Dad."

"Be home early, hon. Ye have a long day tomorrow and ye will have to help Mom. We've a big crowd coming for dinner. She's in bed already."

They walked a long way together hand in hand. She kissed him as often as he wanted in the shadows between the streetlights. Bobby, ever mindful of Marie's well-known admonition about her breasts, was careful to keep his hands from wandering, although that only made his desire more intense. All in all, it was a pleasant night for both of them. He told her a lot about Sarge and Manny, mostly about Sarge. She was amazed and proud of him when he told her about him saving Sarge's life. She told him about her new job as a secretary at the Boston Edison, which she liked a lot. They promised to see each other the next day before and after dinner.

Both the Mohegan's and the Callahan's houses were popular places on Thanksgiving Day in South Boston. Bobby Mo and Marie were the center of attention so all they could manage was a couple of minutes on the phone in the late afternoon. On Friday and Saturday, they found time to hit the wartime Boston scene with a couple of high school friends who had managed to make it home from wherever they were in those dire days. But on both days, Bobby couldn't help feeling that Marie seemed to welcome others to join them wherever they went or whoever they were with. Marie said she'd be the one to drive Bobby into Boston early Sunday morning. It was only a fifteen-minute drive at that hour, but her dad had to go along so she'd have company on the way back. He'd be growling about getting up so early, but he'd do it for her, he said. Maybe they could make it back in time for the 10:00 a.m. Mass at the Gate of Heaven church.

*****

Manny Lopes was greeted exuberantly when the door on the third floor flat on Madero Street flew open. So warmly, in fact, that he began to cry as he was dragged inside by his family.

"*Feliz día* de acción de gracias!" they all shouted in unison. "Happy Thanksgiving Day!"

He was kept prisoner for the next three days. The expat Mexican community in the neighborhood flocked to see and hear the young *soldada* (soldier) they sent off to war just a few months ago. He told the young ones huddled googly-eyed at his feet about shooting guns and marching everywhere. He told them about his new friends, Bobby Mo and Sarge. Only with his father, in rare moments they had alone, did he try to explain the scene at the shooting range. He never mentioned that it was his warnings about Richard Chesterfield that led to Bobby Mo's quick response and the subsequent bond between the three of them. It was, of course, difficult for his father to totally grasp the relationships but he sensed that whatever had happened was good for his son. That was enough for him.

CHAPTER 11

A T 6:00 A.M. ON SUNDAY morning in Pawtucket, Rhode Island, Andrew loaded his gear into Tommy's 1940 Plymouth sedan. An hour later, Marie and her father pulled up at the Mohegan house in a 1939 Ford two-door sedan at the same time Manny and his father started up the latter's 1938 Ford pickup. They all headed separately for Downtown Boston as the sun began to rise over Boston Harbor, promising a crisp fall morning.

They arrived almost simultaneously at 7:30 a.m. at the bottom of Park Street near the corner of the Common. Sergeant Rick O'Brien was nowhere to be seen. They found a parking spot on Tremont Street and were soon out of their cars to introduce themselves to the ones they hadn't yet met. As Andrew approached Marie, he was struck by her stunning beauty. The early morning sunlight seemed to amplify the redness of her hair and the pearly whiteness of her face. Even though she was wearing a velvet wool coat against the cold, Andrew could tell that she possessed a body that would seem to welcome a man's arms.

Marie turned away from Bobby Mo to greet Andrew. She did not hear Bobby say, "Marie, this is Sarge, Sgt. Andrew Vitkus, the guy I've been telling you about. The guy, you know, on the shooting range. I mean, I shouldn't say that I…"

As Marie's right hand was enveloped by Andrew's, she felt weak instantly. She usually cast her eyes downward in the process of meeting any male over the age of eighteen for the first time. This time, she did not. Her eyes held Andrew's for only a few seconds. But her heart began to beat wildly. He held her hand too long.

Bobby Mo noticed, "Hey, guys, you two know each other or something?"

A loud honking startled everyone. Sergeant Rick had arrived with the big Buick. The three men scrambled to say good-bye to their loved ones. Everyone was crying, except Rick who had done his share of it with his wife and two kids two hours ago. The three men first piled their gear into the Buick then turned for last goodbyes before heading south. Bobby Mo bear-hugged Marie's dad and then turned to Marie. She kissed him solidly enough and told him to be careful, that she'd write to him. "Please write me, Bobby Mo." But it wasn't enough and he didn't know why.

Andrew reached for Marie's hand, and held it firmly this time, and brushed her cheek with his. Then he took the chance offered him. "You are really beautiful," he whispered to her. "Just like Bobby said. I hope I can…"

"Thank you," she said. Their eyes locked again but only for a moment this time.

Andrew turned to thank Tommy for the ride up. "Not bad looking there, brother," was Tommy's reply.

"Who?"

"You know who."

Andrew climbed into the front seat, trying to get a last look at Marie. He thought she was looking for him but he wasn't sure. He also wanted to do serious damage to Tommy's fading face as the big Buick took off down State Street.

*****

Outside of making sure that Rick knew the way out of the city and onto route 1, there wasn't much chatter among the four soldiers as they headed south. Each of them was lost in his own thoughts. They knew what they had experienced the past few days would have to last them for a long time.

Bobby Mo finally spoke up, "So, Sarge, how was your dad? Is he going to be all right? By the way, who drove you up from Pawtucket? I thought you said you had a friend here in Boston?"

"Bobby, I don't know. My dad looks pretty sick. I'm sure he's not going to last too long. The other guy is my brother, Tommy. My half brother." He ended it there and no one pressed him further about their relationship or about the absent friend from Boston.

Then all of them opened up about the good times each just had. All morning, they commented on the concerns each family had about the war. The one message they had been given over and over was the hope that the war would end quickly and that these four loved ones would not have to engage in combat. That they would come home unscathed. As the miles piled up, the conversation began to fall off. Every once in a while though, one of the backseat passengers would make an effort to make sure that Sergeant O'Brien wouldn't fall asleep at the wheel.

"Are you OK, Sergeant?"

"Not sleepy, are you, sir?"

Until the sergeant turned back to them and said, "Knock it off, guys. I'm wide awake!"

Sergeant Vitkus hardly talked or engaged in any conversation. Mostly he thought about Marie. He had known a few women here and there but she was different somehow. He was stunned at the way she had let him hold her hand so long and how she looked directly into his eyes. He wondered if he was entirely mistaken about the meaning of the flirtation, if that was what it was, or if it even suggested a future relationship. Finally, the Buick rumbled over the George Washington Bridge.

"No toll for you, Sergeant. Go get those Japs!"

The toll taker's words jolted Andrew into reality, He turned to the boys in the back, his left arm resting on the top of his seat. He looked directly at them as much as he was able then he spoke in a stage whisper. "Even Rick here doesn't know what I'm going to tell you. It's only a strong rumor so far among the NCOs. We heard that we're all going to be issued summer wear and even tropical wear in the next week or so."

"*Wow!*" exulted Bobby Mo. "I never did like cold weather. I'm gonna get me some Japs!"

"Quiet, Bobby!" interrupted Manny. "It's only a rumor. Besides, from what I hear, the Japanese ain't gonna surrender that easily. I'll bet the war won't be over 'til June there."

"Bobby," said Sarge, trying to get his attention, "you may want to go somewhere where it's warm. But I was at Guadalcanal, that's an island we captured in the Pacific with the marines' help." He laughed sarcastically before continuing, "That's where I got so sick they had to deadhead me home. Hot! It's so hot there, Bobby. I hope I never see the Pacific Ocean again in my life."

"I hope it's Europe," said Manny. "Everything's going good from what I read. They'll be in Germany soon. We could be home by spring if we went there."

"Too cold!" said Bobby Mo as he slumped back in his seat.

What none of them in the Buick knew or even suspected—for that matter, what no one in the Allied High Command knew or even suspected—was that almost four thousand miles away in Eagle's Nest in Berchtesgaden, Germany, Adolph Hitler was assembling his generals at that very moment to tell them of his audacious plan to surprise the British and American armies rapidly advancing toward Germany through Belgium and France, with a massive counterattack by the Wehrmacht through the supposedly impassable Ardennes forest. Finally, the big Buick arrived at barracks 124B.

"OK, guys, here we are. The place hasn't changed much since we've been gone. I think we all owe Rick here a couple of bucks each for gas. Rick, thanks for the ride."

"Yeah, thanks, Sergeant. Thanks, Rick."

"OK, boys, we still got a lot of work to do to get you in top shape for graduation. Hit the sack early."

"What day is that again, Sarge?" said Bobby Mo.

"Wednesday, December 20. You guys are lucky. You're gonna have twelve weeks of basic under your belts. I only got eight three years ago."

"That's Christmas week, Sarge! You think there's a chance we can get home for Christmas?"

"Not a chance in hell. No family members at graduation either. See you all early tomorrow."

When they resumed work the next morning, it took only minutes for Bobby Mo and Manny to conclude that Sergeant Vitkus was no longer their friend. In fact, he seemed to have become their enemy.

"Lopes, you're moving too slow. Double-time for the next ten minutes!"

"Sir?"

"You heard me, get on it!"

"Mohegan! Just 'cause you were a hero last week doesn't make you one this week. Twenty push-ups right now!"

When Manny and Bobby Mo saw each other at lunch, Bobby was the first to mention the turnabout. "That dirty rat, Manny!"

"I know, *amigo*, but he kind of had to act that way with us, you know?"

"Yeah, I'm not going to save his life next time." They both laughed convulsively, tears running down their cheeks.

*****

The days ticked off slowly. Three weeks went by. Sergeant Vitkus avoided personal contact with the two boys as much as possible. He had a hundred or so others to help get in top shape before graduation. He almost put the late John Mohegan out of his cluttered mind in favor of Marie Callahan. He told himself he had to get her out of his mind just as he had tried to do unsuccessfully of the memory of what he had done to John Mohegan for three years. Now with Mr. Mohegan's son under his wing, the kid having just saved his life, and Marie on his mind all the time, he began to lose focus. His attitude, his whole demeanor had become noticeable to Sergeant O'Brien at the NCO club on Friday night.

"Andy, you OK? You look like you just lost your best friend. We're going somewhere in a week or so. You gotta be ready. And your boys too, they gotta be ready. By the way, your guys get their tropical gear yet?"

"I'm OK, Rick. It's just…I dunno. My guys are gonna see the quartermaster tomorrow." Then he laughed. "Bobby Mo. You know

Bobby Mo. He's so excited. He hates cold weather so much. He's glad we're going to the Pacific. I'm not. I'd rather not head back there. Those Japanese soldiers are warriors, I'll tell you that."

*****

Saturday, December 16 was a cold day in New Jersey. The temperature was 30 degrees, wind 25 mph with gray skies and maybe snow later. Many of the men were taking advantage of two days off in a warm barracks with its wood-fired stoves blazing at both ends and in the middle. They lazed about, writing letters or reading. One of them had a radio, he was listening to Guy Lombardo's orchestra when the station announcer broke in with news:

> *We have just been told that the German army in Belgium has mounted a major offensive thrust against Allied armies in the Ardennes forest, the site of a major battle in World War I. We have no further information at this time. Now back to Guy Lombardo…*

"Hey, guys!" the soldier announced. "I just heard here that the Nazis are mounting a major offensive against the Allies in France!"

"So what?" was the response from the scattered few close enough to hear him. "We're gonna go finish off the Japs!"

CHAPTER 12

OVER THE NEXT FEW DAYS, the entire base was abuzz as rumors and newspaper reports about the Nazis' stunning offensive became major news. Within days, radios and newspapers everywhere were reporting that three German armies, totaling a quarter million troops, were overwhelming the American army's 106th Division as its battle-weary troops tried to defend places no one in America had ever heard of, places like St. Vith in Belgium and Bastogne in France.

Even though the bookie from Brooklyn was still giving three-to-one odds on the Pacific and six-to-one on Europe, those close to the higher-ups began to sense that they were going to Europe and that they would be moving out soon. The first sure indicators was the cancellation of the graduation ceremony. Then came orders for each man in the camp to be issued cold weather gear. That sealed it. A certain tension seized everyone. A thousand new soldiers were gripped by the sudden realization that they were about to go somewhere from which they might never return.

Bobby Mo continued to send off letters to Marie daily. When he had time and was willing to stand in line for a long time, he managed to make a few collect calls to her on the PX phone. One conversation, in particular, startled him. Toward the end of it (with the guy behind him breathing down his neck), Marie asked him what Sarge was doing. That, in itself, was not surprising, but she referred to him by his given name, Andrew.

"Andrew?" he said. "How did you know Sarge's first name? I always call him Sarge when I talk to you about him."

She tried to be casual. 'Oh, I dunno, Bobby. Somewhere along the line, you must have mentioned it to me. He seemed real nice when I met him for a minute that morning."

Bobby held back. He said no more, but he wondered.

In spite of all he had to do to get his men ready to ship out, Sarge also had to get Marie off his mind. In the end, he came to realize he was helpless.

*****

On the 19th of December, the order came. They were to ship out the next morning. They were going first to New York City and then presumably overseas to Europe. A long line formed for the phone at the PX immediately after they were dismissed at 1600 hours.

When Bobby Mo saw it, he realized his best chance would be to come back. So he and Manny whiled away a few hours with a bunch of their bunkmates, playing cards in the barracks and checking and rechecking their gear. Finally, he heard from a friend that the line was down to a dozen or so. He knew he'd better get in it quickly. After only fifteen minutes of waiting, at 2200 hours and over a bad connection, he heard Marie's voice. They both cried a little as he explained what was about to happen. "I can't believe I won't be able to hear your voice for I don't know how long," he cried.

"Me too," she said.

"Maybe when we get to where we're going, I'm not supposed to tell you where, then I can call you. Anyway, the guy behind me is nudging me to hang up. I love you, Marie."

"Me, too," she replied unconvincingly. "Be careful, Bobby."

Sergeant Vitkus was at his wit's end. He couldn't pull away from his duties in order to stand in line for a phone in the NCO club. Besides, he didn't have Marie's number, didn't know where she worked (maybe at the Edison Company?), didn't know quite where she lived other than it was two streets away from Bobby Mo, and didn't know what time of day was best to call her. He also didn't have any clear idea what to say if and when he got her number if she answered the phone. On the last night at the NCO club after dinner with Rick and several fellow sergeants, he suddenly decided on an idea that would give him at least a chance to talk to Marie before he headed to Europe.

"Bobby Mo lives on C Street," he said to himself, "I know that from listening to him mention it a hundred times. Since he said Marie lives just two streets away, then she must live on either A or E Street. That is, if they go alphabetically."

He had already ruled out the possibility of trying all the Callahans in South Boston to find her. That would be an impossible task in an Irish community. Then there was the likely chance of having the wrong person in the Callahan household pick up the phone. Did she have kid brothers or sisters? Bobby probably told him but he couldn't remember. Eventually, he told himself that if he didn't talk to her before he went overseas, he would never talk to her. He would always be tormented by what he thought passed between them at their very short encounter on the streets of Boston two days after Thanksgiving. He abruptly excused himself from his buddies and almost ran to the pay phone area. There were three. One was not being used. He wasn't quite sure how to proceed. To his astonishment, he saw several phone books scattered about. One said "Boston, Massachusetts, and surrounding area." He thumbed through it frantically and found the section marked South Boston. He scrolled through the Cs and found dozens of Callahans. His heart was beating. Then there it was, Michael B. Callahan, 250 E Street, South Boston. *E Street! Two streets away from C Street.*

Some mysterious force told him that the next few moments were going to be very important in his life! He told himself that if he didn't hear her voice in the next few moments, he would never hear it. He had to make the call collect. The pay phone, contrary to its name, didn't take coins. The operator placed the call. The phone rang loudly. It was answered by a young female voice, not Marie's.

"This is a collect call for Marie from Andrew. Will you accept the call?"

"Dad, there's some guy on the phone asking for Marie. What shall I tell him?"

Off in the distance, he heard a muffled voice, "It must be Bobby Mo. Again! Go get her. She's in the kitchen."

"OK, but it doesn't sound much like Bobby. Marie! Phone for you!"

Heart-stopping moments passed until he heard a female voice say, "Hello."

"Will you accept a call from Andrew?" said the operator.

"Yes! Yes! Yes! Andrew. Oh god! I was beginning to think you weren't going to call. I was beginning to think the whole thing wasn't real. For days, all I've thought about is you—"

"Marie, I—"

"And then I said to myself, maybe the way he looked at me and held my hand and told me I was beautiful wasn't real. Was it real, Andrew?"

"Marie, I—"

"My heart almost stopped when I looked at you. I always knew I'd know instantly when I saw the man I wanted to marry. Are you that man, Andrew?"

"MARIE! Stop talking! I can't believe this is happening to me either. I fell in love with you in some crazy way when Bobby showed me your picture and you looked so much like my mother. But when I saw you standing there that morning, I was stunned. You are so beautiful. Look, Marie, we're going at this way too fast. You hardly know me. I hardly know you. But I do want to know you—"

"I want to get to know you too, Andrew. And I feel so bad about poor Bobby. I love him but only as a good friend. He's such a wonderful guy."

"You don't have to tell me, Marie. I know he is. He's the best!"

"Look, Andrew. I'm going to give you my address at the Edison. Please write me there. I don't want Dad to—"

"I know, Marie. Bobby Mo."

Twenty minutes of conversation bordering on intimacy later, Andrew heard her father's voice in the background, up close this time. "Marie, is that a collect call? I'm not made of money, ye know. Tell Bobby I said hello."

"Marie, I'm going to say this slowly so you'll realize it wasn't a dream. I love you, I want to marry you. I know that's crazy. You're only nineteen. I'm only twenty-one."

"I love you too, Andrew…I think."

"You think?"

"I know. But I've got to be careful with Polish boys. Wait until Dad hears that I'm in love with a Polish boy named Vitkus. I know how to spell it, Andrew. Bobby told me. And here I am lying to my father about who I was talking to. Father O'Connor will surely see me at 7:00 a.m. Mass in the morning. "Oh, Andrew, Andrew! I almost forgot, Merry Christmas."

"Me too, Marie. Merry Christmas to you and the family. I hope to meet soon. Good night, I love you!"

Andrew sank almost to his knees as soon as he hung up. He was crying and laughing at the same time. Then he pushed himself upright and rejoined his NCOs who looked at him for an indication of what the long call was about. "My father," he said as nonchalantly as he could muster. They knew he was lying.

CHAPTER 13

THE TROOP SHIP *EDMUND P. Alexander* sailed from the Port of New York at 1600 hours on December 20, 1944. It was carrying four thousand soldiers and a merchant marine and US Navy crew of two hundred. Its destination, although unknown to its passengers at the time, was Cherbourg, a city on the northwest tip of France across the English Channel from England. Ironically, "*the Alex*," as it soon became referred to by the newly recruited GIs was built in Germany in 1905 as a passenger liner, and seized by the U.S. in New York Harbor at the outbreak of the war. Naturally, the high-end accoutrements it afforded its passengers in peacetime were gone. The soldiers slept in bunks stacked eight high. Bobby Mo gleefully accepted the bottom one while Manny had to climb up to the top each night. Where Sarge slept, they never knew except that his accommodations "must be better than ours."

The Alex made several crossings of the Atlantic by December 1944. In fact, the U-boat threat had been severely diminished by the convoy system adopted by the Allies in 1943. In spite of assurances by the navy personnel on board that "nothin is gonna happen," most of the soldiers were worried that they might end up in the frigid waters of the Atlantic Ocean and be lost in a so-called watery grave. They were required to exercise daily and attend refresher classes taught by soldiers who had already seen combat. One of them was Sgt. Andrew Vitkus who opened up his talk by apologizing for the fact that his combat experience occurred in the South Pacific.

"Most of what I've got to say, unfortunately, won't apply to where we're going. But I'll do my best.

Bobby Mo, although he was proud that "his" sergeant had been asked to lead one of the talks, was a little put off by the session he and Manny attended. "Manny, don't you think it would have been a little better if he had talked about his own experiences rather than all those other guys he talked about?"

"Bobby, cut it out. He was great. He wasn't a bit nervous up there. He's a sound public speaker."

"I guess so. But I wonder what he did on that island…Guada…?"

"Canal."

"Oh yeah."

*****

It was difficult to make the time pass quickly on the old ship as it plowed through the rough seas of the North Atlantic at fifteen knots. To spice up the deadening routine, most of the troops looked forward to Christmas Day. It fell on a Monday so the wise-asses proclaimed it a *long weekend*. "No work until Tuesday!" they announced.

But a couple of days before Christmas, a mimeographed flyer made its way into all hands on board, announcing a special Christmas dinner on Monday at 1800 hours, "Volunteers are needed to help serve. Report to your mess hall at 1600 hours." Dinner was to be served in four separate mess halls as close to the appointed time as possible. No K-rations. This was going to be the real thing. Gifts of candy bars, smokes, and dried fruit as well as emotional handshakes, hugs, and Merry Christmases were exchanged spontaneously by the soldiers early on Christmas Day. All the food was canned, of course, but the quartermaster planned well for the day. Steaming hot turkey, ham, potatoes, cranberry sauce—all was gobbled up as soon as it was served by the volunteers who cheerfully announced that they "got theirs earlier."

Manny and Bobby Mo gave each other long hugs. In their short time of acquaintance, they knew they would be friends forever and their wordless hugs seemed to reflect that promise.

Then over the loudspeakers in each mess hall came a stern voice. "Gentlemen, quiet please." Over and over and louder and louder, it repeated until only a low buzz could be heard over the rocking ship. "Gentlemen, good evening and Merry Christmas to you all. I hope you all can hear me. My name is Colonel Ashby Williams."

Bobby Mo and Manny exchanged looks. "That's the guy who was on the shooting range that day with the general."

"I hope you've had a good Christmas dinner. Not as good as Mom would make at home, we all know that. But the entire staff of wonderful cooks and servers did their best to make this a great Christmas Day. Didn't they?" Cheers and applause. "However, I'm here to hand the microphone to a man whom I gladly serve as adjunct and who I will continue to serve in combat in the weeks and months ahead in Europe. His name is Brigadier General Avery McDonald." Manny and Bobby Mo looked at each other again with knowing smiles. "The general is here to bring one of you a special Christmas gift, but I'll let him take the mic."

General McDonald took the mike and went through a long list of things they all should be grateful for, which was received with perceptible groans and almost audible, "Oh, shut up's."

"Now to the task at hand as the Colonel mentioned. Where is Sgt. Andrew Vitkus? Where is the sergeant? Over there, I see. Come on up here, Sergeant."

Bobby Mo and Manny and all their platoon mates sat up straight and stared at each other. Their mouths were open. "What the hell was going on?"

The two of them couldn't make out Andy across the room. If they were near him they would have seen an astonished man surrounded by astounded fellow NCOs trying to come to grips with whatever was about to happen. His buddies pushed and prodded Andrew whose face showed that his heart was pounding loudly. "Get up there!" they said.

"Gentlemen. This man who's coming up here reluctantly, I see, has no idea what I am about to do. As the colonel said, I'm going to give the sergeant a Christmas present. I've had it for two days, it came as a cablegram, but I held it until tonight. Here he is, Sgt. Andrew Vitkus!" Andrew was beginning to realize what might be happening but he dared not say it to himself in case it wasn't what he thought it might be. "Some of us in these rooms, on this ship, have already seen combat. I have. So has my adjutant over there. A few of you have been shot at or have shot at the enemy yourselves. Sergeant Vitkus has seen combat. I'm here tonight to present to Sgt. Andrew Vitkus a special Christmas gift." Not a sound anywhere now on the rolling ship. No buzz. Nothing. "Sgt. Andrew Vitkus, I am proud to announce to all these soldiers and I'm proud to present to you the Silver Star Medal for gallantry in action against an enemy of the United States, named the so-called Japanese Kingdom, in Guadalcanal on the 18th of August, 1942."

The entire audience exploded to its feet, cheering and clapping as the general recounted Andrew's deeds that day over two years ago. When they finally quieted down, many of them were crying. Bobby Mo and Manny were surrounded by their friends who were congratulating them as if they had been the recipients. By this time, most everybody in their platoon and even the whole company knew that a special relationship existed between the three of them. Indeed, some often wondered how that relationship would play out later in combat.

When things had quieted down, the general continued, "You know, as a person who's in charge of a thousand men, it's impossible for me to know many of you personally. But as the sergeant here knows, I've met him once before. Haven't I, Sergeant?" Then the general began to describe the scene at the shooting range on that almost dreadful day. Of course, Richard Chesterfield's name was omitted. "And I know that young man who saved Sergeant Vitkus from sure death that day is here tonight. I certainly hope he is. What's his name, Sergeant? "Oh yeah, Pvt. Robert Mohegan from a place called Southie or something like that. And he's got a nickname. What is it, Sergeant? Bobby Mo? That's right, Bobby Mo. Come up here, Bobby Mo! Your Christmas gift. There he is! Let me shake your hand again. Your gift is a promotion, in front of all these guys, to corporal."

What a night! What a Christmas! What no one seemed to notice was the long and seemingly serious conversation that took place off to the side between the general and Sergeant Vitkus and the broad smile evaporating on Andrew's face as he walked away from the general. As he accepted congratulations from the crowd, Andrew desperately sought out Bobby Mo. When he found him, he asked, "Where's Manny? I need to talk to him."

"He's over there, Sarge, Cleaning up. I think he volunteered for KP. He's crazy. What a great guy."

It was difficult to push through the well-wishing crowd but Andrew finally found Manny. He was dumping garbage into barrels. "Food for the fishes, Sarge. Congratulations! None of us knew about all that stuff you did—"

"Manny, listen to me. I didn't know that Bobby Mo was gonna be promoted tonight in front of everybody. I wanted to tell you both together."

"Tell us both together what, Sarge?"

"That you're both getting promoted. Congratulations, Manny! You're a corporal too. Only you and Bobby and I knew about you picking up on Chesterfield's craziness. If you hadn't told Bobby to be alert, that nut would have got me good!"

"But, Sarge," said Manny with a mischievous grin, "you still would've got the Silver Star, only posthumously." They both laughed so hard that curious soldiers around them thought they was passing on the latest dirty joke.

*****

On the morning of December 28, the general spoke again over the loudspeakers. This time, his tone was grave. "Gentlemen, I know you're all anxious about what's going to happen next. Well, tomorrow at 0800 hours, we're going to dock at a town in France called Cherbourg. It wasn't a direct landing site for D-Day, but it became important to us, the Brits and the U.S., as a shipping port for men, materials, and supplies a few months ago. The Germans tried to destroy it so the Allies couldn't use it. It's in bad shape but we'll be able to get in there all right. Before you know it, you'll be off to your destination. Your—our destination is a little town 750 kilometers or about 450 miles away. It's called St. Vith, a small town in Belgium. Our troops captured it. The Germans now occupy it again. Our goal, and we'll be attached to the 106th Infantry Division, will be to help them recapture it. It's gonna be awfully cold. I don't know how far we'll be driven. The one road is in god-awful shape from what I hear. So you might have to hoof it at times. Me too, by the way. You've all been trained well. Good luck. See you tomorrow."

There was no cheering, no applause at the end of the general's talk this time. Some of the usual malcontents muttered things like, "It's gonna be a cold day in hell before I'll see him walking with us!"

In later years, they would reminisce about the cold day in Belgium when they saw General McDonald on a ruck march with his troops on the way to St. Vith. By New Year's Day, they made it by truck about twenty miles away from St. Vith, where the booming of the big guns made many of them shiver more from the sounds than from the cold. They knew it might be only a few days or even hours before they would be in combat.

Sergeant Vitkus had disappeared but he joined them out of nowhere. "I got a lift for a few miles." He grinned at their astonishment and greeted Bobby Mo and Manny as corporals.

"Hey, Sarge! What's up?" said Manny. "We haven't seen you since the ship unloaded. Somebody said you looked upset or something. You OK?"

"Yeah, I'm OK, Manny. The top brass keep bugging me. The general went after me the other night. They want me to go home, to deadhead me from Cherboug like they did when I was sick in Guadalcanal. I'm supposed to help sell war bonds or something because I got the medal. I don't wanna go so I'm ducking them as much as I can."

"Why, Sarge? Why?" asked Manny. "You've been through it all. No one's gonna think less of you if you go back to the States. Of course, we'll miss you," he said, nodding toward Bobby Mo who hadn't said a word since Sarge pulled up.

"Manny,"—he kept his voice down so only Manny could hear—"honestly, I've got a great platoon, especially with you and Bobby Mo. I wanna make sure you two make it home all right."

Andrew Vitkus still desired to tell Bobby Mo that it was he who cut John Mohegan's life short on a sidewalk in Boston over three years ago and still hadn't found the courage to confess to Mr. Mohegan's only son, fearing the consequences. He knew if he went home now, the opportunity would be gone forever. He also knew he had to tell Bobby that in a moment of spontaneous ecstasy, he had fallen in love with Marie Callahan and she with him. Andrew wanted to address both situations before they went home or before one of them would *not* come home. Bobby Mo was unusually quiet at the sight of the sergeant. Andrew began to march alongside him. "What's up, Bobby? You OK? Cold enough for you? You wanted to go to the Pacific as I remember. How are you doing with the cold?"

"OK, Sarge. When I get home, I think I'll take up skiing. Say, Sarge, I bumped into one of your buddies yesterday. I won't tell you which one. He told me the good news."

The good news? thought Andrew. He knew about the medal. He asked, "About what? The Medal?"

Bobby looked straight ahead. "No, not about the medal. About your girlfriend. He said you told him you were in love." Andrew suddenly felt very cold. He began to shiver involuntarily. "We didn't hear about that Sarge, Manny and me. You always tell us about those things. The guy who told me that she was from Boston, the girl."

Andrew took one last shot at evasive action. "You don't believe everything you hear, do you, Bobby?"

"Nope, but I think I believe this one."

The pace picked up, their breaths condensing in time with each step. Both men looked straight ahead or down at the snow. Neither spoke for ten minutes. Sarge knew now that Bobby knew about Marie. It had to be Rick who told him. He thought back to how Rick knew about Marie.

Damn him! I shouldn't have told him that last night on the ship. At least I should have told him not to tell Bobby Mo. I guess I forgot. Damn me!

Snow was swirling around the marching troops now. It was a foot deep and getting deeper. Most of the men were thinking about where they were going to bivouac for the night or even if they would have to engage in their first combat without sleep at all.

Bobby Mo was seething. He knew now that the man he trusted since the first day at Fort Dix whose life he saved on the range had somehow betrayed him. And Marie! How could she? It seemed impossible. But the way Rick excitedly told Bobby that it all happened in a flash and Rick, not one to betray a friend in the excitement surrounding the Silver Star award, had temporarily forgotten Bobby's relationship with Marie. "So, Sarge," asked Bobby Mo with all the sarcasm and resentment he could muster, "are you in love with a girl from Boston? I didn't know you knew any girls from Boston."

Ten or so paces more, and Andrew would have had to answer, but the sound and the shock from a German long gun's shell exploding in the field seventy-five yards away knocked them off their feet and into the soft snow. They struggled back to their feet only to hit the ground again as all the soldiers in their vicinity simultaneously dived for cover. In a few minutes, the troops were back on their feet and headed to St. Vith with renewed purpose, comforted just a little by the words of the few who previously experienced combat that it was probably an errant shot. "There's no point in shooting at us way out here. The bastards probably don't even know we're coming."

Bobby Mo and Sergeant Vitkus resumed marching, also. But this time, as the entire troop moved closer to St. Vith in the face of the blowing snow, they were no longer marching alongside each other.

CHAPTER 14

THE LONG LINE, NOW ONLY ten miles from St. Vith, began to stall on the 5th of January. The Germans still occupied the town and the US Army's XVIII Corps was getting ready to take it back.

While Sgt. Andrew Vitkus was being honored with a Silver Star on Christmas Day on board *the Alex*, troops of the Seventh Armored Division were fighting a losing battle out of St. Vith. The Seventh could not hold against the pressure of six German divisions. The U.S. 106th—the unit Sergeant Vitkus and Bobby Mo and Manny and their companions were about to assist, had suffered substantial loss of life. General Avery McDonald's charges were ordered to leave the battered roadway and to seek cover in a loose group of farm houses, which had been battered by bombs and shells to the extent that they were only twenty or thirty buildings left extant. The general set up his command post in what once was a farmhouse and the troops scattered to find shelter.

Sergeant Vitkus had to work hard to bring his platoon together in a three-room farmhouse that precariously held two-thirds of a thatched roof over their heads. But he finally managed as the sun was setting. The pale orange sky to the west indicated that the snow would give way to a frigid day tomorrow. "OK, boys, this is all we got until who knows when. I imagine we'll be here until a few days before the attack. But we have food, if you can call K-rations food. At least, we have cover against the wind. Make the most of your tents and help each other as much as possible. There are some of your buddies who are more tired than you. Help them so they can help you later."

"Sounds like a commercial, Sarge," said one of the wise guys.

"It was," was the reply.

Bobby Mo and Manny cleared off a space on the floor of what was once a kitchen and sat against a stone wall that was laid three centuries before. They said very little for a while. Then Bobby Mo spoke up. "You hear any news about Sarge?" Manny didn't respond. "So you know about him and Marie?" Again, no response. "You deaf or something?"

"No, I'm not deaf. What do ya want me to say?"

"I want you to tell me what you know about that man I thought was my friend, maybe my friend for life, taking my girlfriend away from me. Who told you? Rick?"

"Yes."

"Manny, how could that have happened? I mean, as far as I knew, they only saw each other once for a few minutes the morning we left. I heard he fell in love with her picture. I never should have showed it to him. I mean, how could he fall in love with a picture? He said it looked like his mother. Why didn't he marry his mother?"

"Bobby, stop it! How do I know? You're talking crazy. Get some sleep."

"I can't sleep!"

"You're gonna have to."

*****

January 21 was a Sunday. At 0700 hours, a Roman Catholic Mass was held at the bottom of a small hill away from the buildings. The altar was a pile of rocks, the remainder of a stone wall that probably served as a property line for centuries. It was bitterly cold and windy as hundreds of men shuffled and stamped their feet and tried to listen to the middle-aged chaplain, who was obviously from the Bronx by the way he invited them to join him afterwards for "corfee," deliver a short sermon about the crucifixion of Jesus. During the Mass, he was assisted by several soldiers who distributed the Holy

Communion wafers, which, in the Roman Catholic tradition, represent the body and blood of Jesus. The men, whether they were spiritually encouraged or not by the Mass, clearly now knew that the effort to arrange for it to happen was a sure sign they were about to go into action very soon.

"We're going tomorrow for sure," said Manny. "The tanks keep rolling by over there." He pointed to the faraway road.

"Manny, did you notice that Sarge didn't go to the Mass or take Communion like you and I did? I mean, shouldn't he have, like all the rest of us? He's Polish so he must be Catholic—"

"Bobby Mo, Stop this right now! If you don't get over the Marie thing *now*…If you don't get Sarge out of your mind, you're gonna get yourself killed. And worse, you're gonna get *me* killed. I don't wanna get killed! I wanna go home in good shape. You hear me? If you keep it up, I'm gonna report you up the line and the war will be over for you, just like it is for Chesterfield. You hear me?"

Bobby Mo was chastened. To be put in a class with Chesterfield stung him. He had never heard Manny talk to him or to anybody like that. He knew he had allowed his thoughts to become vengeful toward Sarge and not on getting himself totally ready for combat.

*****

St. Vith was a small marketplace town in Belgium founded in the twelfth century. It had been almost completely destroyed by the bombing and the big guns from both sides since mid-December. They moved into it after dark on January 23. Most of the main German army had moved on. Even as they retreated, the enemy left behind in the crumpled ruins of the old city pockets of resistance to hold off the Americans and slow down their inevitable advance.

"We're fresh troops. Everybody ahead of us is tired and worn out. We've got to go in and weed out those bastards with the machine guns so the city can be cleared out once and for all," Sergeant Vitkus told his platoon the next morning at 0530 hours.

Bobby Mo spoke up, "Hey, Sarge, what's the name of this place? Saint Vith? Sounds like they named it after you." Bobby Mo joined everyone in laughing at his joke. But it wasn't a joke and Sergeant Vitkus knew it. It was a sign from Bobby Mo that everything was going to be all right.

"I dunno, Bobby. It could be. Us Poles have been all over Europe but none of us were saints, I'll tell you that." More laughter. *Thank you, Bobby Mo*, thought Sergeant Vitkus. *I knew you'd come through for me. Made the rest of the boys a little looser too.*

The city was eerily silent as they crept into it. Now and then, a short burst of automatic fire could be heard but the sounds were far enough away to not worry them.

Sergeant Vitkus quietly spoke to his men. "That's where we're going. We've got to knock these guys out. Let's move out and see if we can find them."

An hour later, the staccato bursts of sporadic gunfire from the German machine gunners were loud and clear. A corporal from the 106th met them in the ruins of a small church. "They're about a hundred yards ahead. About a half dozen of them on the roof of a building on the Rue de…something and St. Vith Avenue. You can't miss it. Be careful, they're fanatics. Good luck!"

Bobby Mo was the first one in the platoon to make a move. As soon as he spotted where the firing was coming from, he ran, body bent over, along the narrow street in rubbles, firing from the hip. In spite of the severe cold and biting wind, when he found cover behind a stout stone wall, he was soaking wet from his own sweat.

Sarge joined him in a few minutes, breathing heavily. "You OK, Bobby? You're a crazy man. *Wow!*"

"I'm OK, Sarge. You? As soon as they let up a little bit, Sarge, I'm gonna see if I can lob one in there. They're on the roof. They've got control of this whole entire section. I can knock them out, I know I can. Where's Manny? Do you know?"

"*Jeez*, Bobby! I got the whole platoon to take care of. I…I'm sorry. I know you guys—"

"Sarge, Manny loves you! We gotta make sure he's OK!"

"OK! OK!"

"Sarge, they've let up. I'm going. I've got two grenades. And I've got a great arm, should've made the varsity."

"The what?"

"Never mind. Cover me. Here I go!"

Bobby Mo zigzagged across the open space. No German seemed to see him. He didn't fire as he ran, crouching low. He was ten yards away when he threw the first grenade. It hit a stone buttress, bounced back, and landed five yards away from him. It was a dud. Lucky for Bobby Mo. It would have done serious damage to him had it not misfired. No one spotted him as he got close to the building. He grabbed a second one from his belt, pulled the pin, and let it fly. This time, the throw was perfect and the effect was instant horror. Bobby was stunned, realizing that he just killed and wounded human beings. He turned and looked for cover. He spotted a small pile of rubble and ran for it.

Sergeant Vitkus provided as much cover for Bobby as he could. A couple of his other men joined him. Except for the screams and moans from the German soldiers who survived the blast, the small town square suddenly become dead silent. Sergeant Vitkus peered carefully over his place of cover and looked for Bobby. He couldn't see him.

"Bobby! Bobby! You OK?" His voice echoed off the walls of the ruined buildings nearby.

"Sarge, I'm hit!" was the plaintive reply.

"Where are you, Bobby?"

"Over here! See my weapon? I'm waving it. I'm hurt bad. I'm bleeding bad!"

"Where?"

"My leg, my left leg! I think I'm bleeding out, Sarge!"

Sergeant Vitkus turned to the two frightened men beside him. "I'm gonna go help him. Give me cover. See if one of you can get the sniper who got him. Call for a medic for Bobby, you hear? You ready? Here I go!"

Andrew ran low and zigzagged the twenty yards toward Bobby's temporary haven. His two platoon members fired simultaneously at where they thought the sniper was hidden. Seconds later, the two men slapped each other around joyously. The sniper had been hit. They had, so to speak, made their bones. In a second, Andrew was next to Bobby. He was bleeding badly but he wasn't bleeding out. Andrew could tell. In the Pacific, he had seen some soldiers who had bled out and they were gone in minutes. He was out of breath from the short run and excitement.

He reassured Bobby Mo, "You aren't bleeding out, but it looks like you have a pretty significant wound. I'm gonna cut off your pant leg to see what it looks like and get a tourniquet on it. The medics will be here in a couple of minutes."

Bobby screamed in pain. The square was silent except for the moans from the roof that eventually ceased. Three medics joined Bobby and Sarge and quickly assessed Bobby Mo's condition, one of them told Sergeant Vitkus what they had to do.

"Sarge, nice job on the tourniquet. He's in a lot of pain. We're gonna give him some morphine, bandage him up as best we can, put him on this sled here, and take him back with us."

One of them leaned in and spoke quietly to Sarge, "This guy's war is over."

"Sarge, where's Manny?" Bobby Mo wasn't knocked out yet.

"I'm not quite sure, Bobby. We'll find him." Then he bent down. In total disregard for every possible army regulation, he clasped Bobby's anguished face between his long hands, looked into his eyes, and said, "Bobby Mo, I love you. You're gonna be all right. You hear?"

"Thanks, Sarge. I know I will. I love you too. Hey, Sarge?"

"Yes, Bobby?"

"Take good care of her. She's such a good girl."

And with that, he was gone, whisked off to the rear. But where was Manny?

One of his soldiers spoke up. "Sarge, when Bobby's grenade went off, I thought I heard a second small blast at the same time. Maybe a trip mine?"

"Where?"

"Well, Manny took after Bobby but he kinda took the long way around. Wait! There he is!"

Sure enough, Cpl. Manny Lopes caught his foot in a trip wire but the blast knocked him into a pile of rocks. He was just coming to when Sarge and a fellow soldier reached hm. He was lying on his back, his head and face bloodied from the fall.

"My god, Manny! You OK? Lucky you weren't killed. Musta been a faulty mine. Bobby got shot in the leg. The medics are taking him to the rear."

Manny was obviously in shock. He could hardly comprehend. "Bobby's dead?"

"No, no, he's just wounded. You got knocked out by a trip mine. The medics are here. They'll help you get up if you can."

"Sarge...?"

"Yes, Manny?"

"I can't seem to move my legs."

On January 23, 1945, World War II ended for corporals Bobby Mohegan and Manny Lopes. Not so for Sgt. Andrew Vitkus. He had a platoon of well-trained soldiers to lead into France and Germany for as long as it would take for the war to end for everyone.

CHAPTER 15

WHAT HAD HAPPENED TO BOBBY Mo and Manny? It was now April 1945, Sergeant Vitkus was continuously worried about the condition and whereabouts of the only two men in his platoon who had been seriously injured in the war and to whom he had irrationally become too close. He also thought continuously about his father who he knew was gravely ill and, of course, Marie. He now rarely thought about John Mohegan. Berlin was about to fall to the Russians and the Allies. The end of the Nazi's thousand-year reign was to occur 990 years earlier than Hitler had predicted.

But where were Bobby Mo and Manny? Finally, Andrew's persistent questioning of medical personnel and higher-ups for information paid off. Bobby Mo had been taken back to the rear to be treated for his wound. Then he was moved to Cherbourg and shipped across the Channel to a rehabilitation hospital in Warwickshire, England. He was scheduled to be shipped home in April but his fate was uncertain. Manny's location was pretty certain. He, too, had been sent to the Rear for preliminary evaluation of what appeared to be a spinal injury caused by the shrapnel from the land mine. He was paralyzed below the waist, a paraplegic. Then Andrew heard for sure that Manny would be transferred soon to Walter Reed Hospital in Washington DC for long-term treatment for his paralysis. As he moved across Germany in the spring of 1945 with the 106th, Andrew thought a lot about the strange events that happened around him since September 1941.

He actually started questioning God. Did *he* exist? If so, did everything that happened to him have a specific purpose or any purpose at all? And Marie. Had what transpired between them so quickly that Thanksgiving weekend on a Boston sidewalk really constitute as "falling in love" event for both of them or was it just one of those times when a man and a woman spontaneously lock eyes across a crowded room with only one thing in mind? Lately, he convinced himself it was the latter. Then came the mail, which caught up with them in a little German town right after the Germany's unconditional surrender on May 8, 1945. In Andrew's first letter to Marie, he had trouble putting his thoughts down on paper. He was too busy with his duties to find the time and he felt guilty about that.

"Hey, Sarge!" called the middle-aged sergeant mail clerk as he dumped a canvas bag full of letters on Andrew's lap one morning in early May. "Who you got sending so many letters? I bet there's a couple of hundred here."

Andrew sat against a wall in shock. It wasn't a couple of hundred, but there were a lot. His heart began beating faster as he shuffled through them. A couple were from his father to whom he had only written twice from Europe and it only had a few lines of encouragement. The rest had a return address listed as the Boston Edison Company. That's where he sent his few letters to her.

"We mustn't let my father find out yet," she had written earlier.

In his letters, he had been careful not to push the relationship on her too strongly:

> *I'm not sure how to address you, Dear Marie? Dearest Marie? My darling? Please tell me.*
>
> *Are you sure? We only saw each other that one time for just a few minutes? I think…I know I'm in love with you. How could that be? You're so beautiful, but I only saw you once. Hah! Joke.*
>
> *I promise I won't go too fast or put too much pressure on you. If you have second thoughts about whether you're in love with me, just let me know!*

Now as he skimmed through hers to him, he was struck by the passion and simple eloquence they exhibited.

> *Andrew, I only saw you once on that cold morning but immediately felt a strong desire for you. Dearest Andrew, how could I fall in love—deeply in love—with a man I hardly know? My love, I want to have children with you. A lot of them. Isn't that crazy?*
>
> *Dear Andrew, sometimes I think I'm losing it. Will I recognize you? Will you recognize me? Do you want me to call you Andrew or Andy or Drew or even Sarge as Bobby calls you? How weird these thoughts of mine. You're on my mind every day as I sit at my desk at work, down by the beach, or at home with Mom and Dad.*
>
> *Please come home safe. Each day at morning Mass, I pray to the Blessed Virgin that you'll come home safe and sound. And Bobby too, of course. And his friend, the one he talked about so much. Manny. I don't remember his last name. I pray he'll come home safe and sound too.*

On May 5, Andrew's unit was stationed a few miles outside Berlin. The Germans surrendered unconditionally three days later. The war was over for them but not for the Allies. The Japanese would go down fighting, everyone knew that. Maybe a year. Maybe more.

As he sat in the morning sunshine on an abandoned bullet-ridden couch with Marie's letters strewn about, he looked around at his men. Although they had seen little action since St. Vith, they were tired. They wanted to go home. But in the back of their collective minds there was one dominating thought: Japan! He couldn't help feel a little superior to Marie's way of thinking. All her praying to the Blessed Virgin—Who was she? Oh, now I remember. When Mom made me go to Sunday school after Mass. She was the mother of Jesus. Well, all three of us will get home "safe" it looks like. But

Manny and Bobby Mo certainly won't come home "sound." God I hope Manny will be able to walk again. *There I go with the God thing again. Gotta stop using that name. Makes me think sometimes that He...Stop it...You don't even believe in God and now here you are giving him a male first name.*

He knew now he was lost in a gender and theological crisis of his own making. So he looked down idly at the last few unopened letters at his feet. He picked one up. It was postmarked February 9 and was a bit bulky. *Maybe a photo of her?* No photo. A newspaper clipping dated February 1, 1945 from the *Providence Journal* fell out.

Local Man Awarded Silver Star

Sergeant Andrew J. Vitkus of Pawtucket was recently awarded a Silver Star for gallantry in action at the battle of Guadalcanal on August 18, 1942. The award was presented to the sergeant at an undisclosed location in Europe.

Sgt. Andrew Vitkus is a graduate of Pawtucket High School, class of 1941. His father, Charles L. Vitkus, told a reporter that he was "all-out proud" of his son.

Marie's letter indicated that she too was "all-out proud" of her future husband.

A guy in work from Rhode Island brought it to me. He overheard me mentioning your name when I talked about Bobby. Maybe I talked a little bit too much about you. I am so proud of you, Andrew. I showed it to everybody and my whole family. They were all happy. But they all looked at me kind of suspiciously, especially my dad. "Nice guy," he said. "Must be brave. But it's not like Bobby Mo won it. Take it easy. He's only a friend of Bobby's. He's not your boyfriend or anything. Have you even met him?"

Andrew, I held my breath, *"Once," I said. "But only for a moment that day they all took off from downtown. You drove me in. You met him too, Dad."*

"Oh yeah," he said.

Andrew, *I think he suspects something. I was too gushy!*

CHAPTER 16

O F THE THREE, MANNY HAD gotten back to the States first on March 1. He received some painful therapy for his legs first at the rear, then in England, and lastly on board the ship. Now he was at Walter Reed Hospital along with a thousand other men who came out of the war safe but not sound.

Bobby Mo was next. After surgery was performed to help transform a gruesome appendage into a working leg again, his first stop in the U.S. was St. Vincent's Hospital in New York City. Marie visited him there on Easter weekend along with his mom and uncle Jim. They came down together by train. Kisses and hugs and "Thank Gods" were exchanged all around. Marie planted a kiss smack on Bobby's eager lips but her eyes told him that the kind of relationship he once thought existed between them would forevermore only be described as platonic.

"Glory be to God, Bobby. This is the first time ever, even when I was a little girl growing up in Galway, that I missed Mass on Easter Sunday. And Jim too," his mother said, smiling at the big Irishman standing happily close to her.

Too close, thought Bobby. He looked up at her from his hospital bed as sternly as his mischievous mind would allow and said in a scolding voice, "My goodness, Mom! You're standing awful close to Uncle Jim. Are you two...?"

The two moved apart at the question. His mother's face flushed rose red in a moment. "Well, Bobby..."—she looked up at Uncle Jim who was grinning like a baboon and then back at Bobby Mo—"Well, it's going on four years since your father died, God rest his soul. Jim had been lonely for ten years since his Theresa's been gone, God rest her soul—"

"Mom, stop! Dad would have loved it. Uncle Jim—I'm still gonna call you that—Is that OK? When's the wedding?"

"We don't know yet," he said. "We were waiting for ye to come home. Weren't we, honey?" Then he caught himself, "Mary?"

Marie and Bobby Mo laughed as the two lovers flushed and grinned like a couple of kids caught kissing behind the hen house. Bobby then asked about Manny. He heard that he had been paralyzed in his legs from the skirmish at St. Vith but not much more about his condition. Marie knew little more about him than that, except to say that his family—all of them—had rented a place in Washington to be near him.

"And how about Sarge, Marie? Have you heard from Sarge?" He hoped his query sounded matter-of-factly.

"I-I heard," she didn't say how, "that Andrew—Sarge will be on the next troop ship to land right here in New York next week. Then he goes off to Fort Dix to be discharged. He…he doesn't have much family so I thought I—"

"You could pick him up yourself? Good idea. Why don't you do that!" Bobby Mo turned to his mother. "Are you folks gonna go out somewhere for dinner or eat here?"

Marie answered for them, "We're going to have it here with you, darling. Aren't we, Mary?"

His mom bounced onto his bed on the good leg side and placed her soft hand on his throbbing chest. "We ordered supper before we came up. So what's this place like, Bobby? Do they treat ye OK?"

Bobby Mo didn't feel much like talking. But he obliged for the next few hours, like the good soldier he had become.

*****

The USS *Breckinridge* pulled into the Port of New York the next week as Marie had predicted, but one of the three thousand passengers was not Sgt. Andrew Vitkus because his company was held back, playing a relatively minor role in the Allies' march across

France and Germany. So it was not until September 7, 1945, that the *Breckinridge* left Portsmouth, England, and headed back across a peaceful Atlantic to bring a motley crew of two thousand soldiers and civilians home to a peacetime America. One of the passengers for sure was Andrew Vitkus who now answered to the call of lieutenant—first lieutenant at that.

On the eight-day voyage, Andrew had little to do except keep control of his newly assigned company. He thought about the future and tried to imagine it. First, he and Marie would go off somewhere and get to know each other better before they took the plunge into marriage. He remembered the admonition she practically posted on her forehead, "No breast touching until the wedding night." He figured that was just a fanciful dream of a fanciful young lady and he would take care of that quickly. Then while he wouldn't mind having a kid or two, more than that would mean trouble. So no more than two.

South Boston didn't appeal to him as a place to live. Too crowded and too much crime, he heard. Maybe for a couple of months then it was off to the suburbs, although he really didn't know what the suburbs were. What to do for a living? He occasionally shook his head hard from side to side to knock the name of one particular occupation out of his mind, police officer. How could a killer become a cop? No one knew that he was a killer, except his father. There was no way Charles Vitkus would tell. Maybe there was one other man who knew though his half brother denied hearing the confession last Thanksgiving. But Tommy was a liar through and through. So, maybe one more. But why a police officer? This is why, he reasoned, he liked the army, liked being in charge, and liked helping people. Deep down, he may have thought that becoming a police officer and fighting crime would offset or maybe be a sort of penance for what he had done. No one knew his secret. Over time, he came to the conclusion that he would never confess to Bobby Mo. What good would it do? One negative thing his confession might do though, even if he never was prosecuted, was destroy the bond the two had developed for each other. So maybe being a cop would be a good job for him.

WHAT DID TED HAVE?

He imagined the question he would be asked at the oral exam. "Mister Vitkus (no regard here for military rank), have you ever been charged with or convicted of a felony? Or any crime?" He would look straight at the stern questioner and he would say, "No, sir!" in the firmest tone ever so that everyone in the room would say, "My, what a great candidate!" Best of all, his answer wouldn't be a lie. Andy rarely lied, although deep down he wasn't quite sure whether repeatedly hiding the fact that he had shot and killed a man a long time ago might be.

*****

On September 15, Andrew and two thousand other happy souls cheered and clapped at the sight of the Statue of Liberty. It took two whole days for disembarking to take place. He was breathing hard with anxiety as he searched frantically for her. In one of her last letters to him, Marie said she'd be wearing a blue dress with a white daisy pattern and a daisy corsage. "So you wouldn't kiss another red-head instead."

Finally, there she was. She was across the street at a parking lot, a long way from the place where the *Breckinridge* had docked. But he could see that she was limping. He put up his hand to stop her and dashed through honking cars to run to her. He was stunned by her beauty even as she stood mostly on her right leg and kept twisting her left. She was crying.

"What happened, Marie? What happened?"

"I...I was running to meet you and I tripped and fell and scraped my knee. It hurts awful!" She lifted her dress to show him, but all he could see as he bent down to look—as he would admit to her later—was not her scraped knee, but her gorgeous upper leg.

"OK. OK. I think you'll be OK." He pulled her as close to him as her condition allowed, placed his two long hands aside her alabaster face, and kissed her decently for a long time. When she pushed him away, he asked her in a scolding manner why she had worn heels and not flat shoes.

She sniffed and said, "Because, dummy, I wanted to look beautiful for you."

He had nothing to say to that, except, "C'mon, I'll carry you to the car. Is it far away?" Then in a series of runs, in which he alternated carrying Marie and his duffel bag, they made it to her dad's vehicle, a '39 two-door Ford sedan. He was out of breath. "I'll drive," he said. "You got a map to Dix? How far is it?"

"About seventy-five miles," she told him. "I looked it up." Marie got into the passenger seat gingerly. When Andrew put the key into the ignition, Marie stopped him. "Hold it, Andrew. Before we take off, let's see if we can get a few things straight. Right here, not on the road."

"OK," said a curious Andrew.

"Andrew, we have personally known each other for all of half an hour, two minutes up in Boston, a couple of minutes on the phone from Dix (if that counts), and ten minutes right here. Less than half an hour. We really have to find out a lot more about each other before we go plunging ahead. I know I somehow feel you're the right man for me. But how can I be sure? And how do you know I'm the right one for you?" Without waiting, she continued, "Andrew…I think we agreed I should call you that rather than Andy or even Sarge. You're a lieutenant now. You look so handsome. Andrew, I want you to know that my father was out of his mind when I told him that I was in love, madly in love, with a man I've only seen in person for twenty minutes and that I wanted to borrow the second most important thing in his life besides God and his family—his 1939"—she spoke slowly "Ford sedan to go to New York to pick him up." Andrew settled in the driver's seat. All around them, hundreds of cars were being loaded up with duffel bags and happy people were driving away. "Really, Andrew, for some reason, I know right now that it's possible you could get me into bed and then all those dreams I've had since I was a little girl about being still a virgin and then marrying the handsome prince would be dashed forever. But, Andrew, I'm not going to let that happen until…until I am absolutely sure …absolutely sure… that you are the man who can love me and provide for me and take care of as many kids as God will let us have for the rest of my life…"

She paused to wipe the tears from her cheeks, "hopefully in South Boston."

So in one rambling passionate discourse about her hopes and dreams for the future years, Marie shattered Andrew's shipboard manifesto before it ever went public. He looked directly into her watery eyes. He took both of her soft hands into his and felt a warmness he had never felt before in his short life. He surrendered without resistance. "Where do I sign up?" he said. "Only one thing, I want to tell you what I want to do for a living." He told her about his desire to become a police officer but he offered no coherent explanation for it.

She smiled and told him that if that was what he truly wanted, she would not object. "It's probably going to be a lot safer than what you've just been through." By the way, she continued, "I was waiting for the right time to tell you. Your father is looking forward to seeing you. We'll see him on the way back."

"My father? What do you mean? How could you have seen my father, Marie? You don't even know where I live—"

"Andrew, that newspaper clipping about the Silver Star gave me all I needed to get started. At work, we had a Pawtucket phone book so I called him and went to see him on the way here. He's a very nice man, Andrew. He doesn't look well though."

"Oh my god! You visited him at home? In that crappy old trailer?"

"Stop it! I've seen worse. We'll stop to see him again on the way back. He's so proud of you."

"You saw my father? You went to see my father? Oh my god! Marie, I love you so much!"

He started the car, moved by Marie's gesture. He drove slowly out of the rapidly emptying parking lot to head to Fort Dix. For the next two hours—which lengthened their time of knowing each other personally to almost three hours—the conversation flowed between them as if they had been sweethearts from childhood. They had not been. But now, it was clear to both of them that they would be, for life.

CHAPTER 17

ANDREW HAD TO REPORT TO Fort Dix to be discharged, which could not be accomplished in one afternoon.

"You will stay in the camp," she said in a commanding tone. "Before that, we will have a nice dinner in a nice restaurant. Then I will get a motel room for myself, you will pay for it. Then to make sure I am not assaulted by some madman or seduced by a first lieutenant, I will lock the door and bolt it from the inside. Is that OK?" Andrew said he'd sit outside her door to guard her against a madman and he knew of no first lieutenant who would do the thing she suggested. "Oh, and you will take me to a nice breakfast place at 7:00 a.m."

She was crying as those last words came out. Sleeping alone in a motel room in New Jersey would actually be frightening to her, but Marie had made a promise to her God a long time ago that she would remain a virgin until her wedding night. Furthermore, she had made the same promise to Mike Callahan. He would know without asking (for he would never ask) whether she had held true to her promise. Many years later, she would confess to her husband that alone in her bed that night, she ached for him so much that if he had knocked on her motel room door at 3:00 a.m., she would have opened it.

At breakfast, they stared at each other for a long time before either spoke a meaningful word.

"I can't believe this." She dabbed her eyes with a napkin.

"I can't either. How could I have met someone like you? All I did was look at your picture."

"And I looked like your mother."

"You did. You do but then you don't. You look so much different. My god, your hair! So red, so beautiful. Bobby said it was brighter than the picture. That's a pretty dress, by the way. I like you in green."

It was days later that he woke up to the fact that she had taken two dresses with her on what was supposed to be a day trip.

*****

They arrived at the trailer in Pawtucket by noon. Charlie moved slowly but he wrapped his arms tightly around his son and around Marie. He was almost a skeleton, his clothes draped over him as if on a hanger. The three of them talked easily. Charlie was entranced by Marie and thrilled by listening to as many of his son's exploits as Andrew would tell him. He was proud that his son was now a first lieutenant and a Silver Star awardee.

In an hour, Andrew realized he could not continue all the way to Boston with Marie to formally meet the Callahans and the Mohegans. He had to stay with his dad. He pulled Marie aside and told her.

"I was going to suggest that, Andrew. He needs you now more than I need you." She stepped back, placed her hand on her bosom, and said in a falsely horrified voice, "Wait a minute! Have I got that right?"

So being formally introduced to Mike Callahan as a future son-in-law would have to wait awhile for Andrew. When the time was right. He kissed and hugged her until she pushed him away. They exchanged telephone numbers.

*****

The next few days were the most emotionally draining of Andrew's life as he reunited with his father. Bathing him, feeding him, and changing the dressings on the sores on his arms and legs was hard to do for this proud young soldier who desperately wanted to get on with his life. But on the other hand, as they talked for hours between the old man's naps, he realized how much they loved each other and his heart became filled with joy. Charles, the prodigal father, apologized again and again for the slipshod life he led during Andrew's teen years. He often cried as he told his son stories about that beautiful redhead he abused so much and whom he greatly missed. Charles gave unstinting approval to Andrew's choice of a bride. But when it came to the subject of John Mohegan's untimely death, he only had one piece of stern advice to give, "Andrew, you must confess to Bobby Mo. He's such a great friend from what you tell me. You told me you want to be a cop. So I guess you'll have to live with that secret if they take you. But from what I hear, Bobby Mo is a fine young man. How's his leg, by the way? When is he getting out of St. Vincent?"

Andrew learned a lot more about Marie through several telephone calls he made to her workplace each day. She constantly reminded him that he was doing the right thing by staying with his father although she longed to be with him.

"By the way," she said on one of their calls, "my dad was pleased that I brought back his precious car in one piece and that I paid for the gas. He was also happy that you were taking care of your father first. At least he's got his priorities straight," she said in a falsetto brogue.

Tommy came by occasionally. He and Andrew were civil to each other. But his father cautioned Andrew one afternoon as he laid on his bed, tethered to an oxygen tank. "Andrew, I'm worried about your brother."

"Half brother, Dad."

"The guys your brother had been hanging with. They're guys from Federal Hill."

"Federal Hill?"

"In Providence. That's where the bad guys hang out. Some real bad guys. I've got a feeling he's doing some things at night that aren't legal. He likes hanging with the mob guys. Please watch out for him."

Andrew said he would, but not in the way his father intended. On Tuesday morning of the second week, Andrew awoke early, kissed his father on the forehead, and went to Rigotelli's to pick up a newspaper and some groceries. When he returned two hours later, he found that Charles Vitkus had slipped away.

"Dammit, Dad!" he said as he kissed his cold forehead, tears rolling down his cheeks. "Just when we were getting to know each other real good. Say hello to Mom. I love you!"

*****

The funeral of Charles Vitkus was attended by two dozen of his AA group plus Tommy and Marie. As she ministered to Andrew in the couple of days leading up to and during the funeral service, Marie was struck by the profound sadness in Andrew's eyes.

At the graveside, he delivered a short but eloquent eulogy, concentrating on his younger years with a happy mother and father. He made no mention of Tommy nor the death of his mother.

"Marie, I wish so much it had been different for the two of us. He was a really good father when I was a little kid. But then it somehow...I dunno...somehow it all evaporated. Then my mother... my mother died and it was all over between him and me. But on Thanksgiving, some of it came back. We had such good talks."

Andrew, of course, didn't tell Marie about his Thanksgiving confession nor did he ever think to compare his anguish to what Bobby Mo's must have been like four years ago. He concentrated on controlling his own thoughts. By now, he had convinced himself that he had driven off his feelings of guilt and was ready to move forward in his life with Marie and whatever the future held for him as a Boston cop, a husband, and maybe a father.

CHAPTER 18

FORMAL INTRODUCTIONS BEGAN A FEW days later in South Boston.

"I'm going to tell ye his straight out," said big Mike Callahan as he enveloped Andrew's large right hand into his even bigger one, "ye had better take care of this wonderful daughter of mine. She's precious to me and to my wife Mary here." But Mike thought he saw the look of an honest man in Andrew's blue eyes. So he was satisfied that Marie found the husband she needed to tame her occasional Irish spirits and to provide him and his wife with as many grandchildren as the couple desired to have.

Andrew did not look forward to meeting Bobby Mo's widowed mother Mary, for obvious reasons. Marie, of course, explained to him that Mary was soon to marry John's brother, Jim. On the way to Mary Mohegan's place, Andrew gave some thought as to whether he should mention her late husband, but he decided not to since it was now four years since John's death.

As she slurped her tea and nibbled at her own "dee-licious" Irish bread, Mary spoke up. "Jim and John were Irish twins, ye know."

Marie, seeing Andrew's perplexity, explained to him that Irish twins were siblings born in the same twelve-month period.

"So, *um*," said Andrew carefully, "Uncle Jim, did you and... your brother...look alike?"

"Yer looking at his spittin' image, Andrew. That's why Mary said yes when I asked her."

"That's not true at all, you old fool. Here, Andrew, let me show you some pictures of my John, God rest his soul," she said as she dabbed at her eyes and pulled out her frayed album of black-and-white photos.

Andrew quietly agreed that John and Jim weren't look-alikes and he felt relieved that he wasn't talking to the ghost of the man he killed.

*****

"Bobby Mo's coming home!" was the cry that echoed up and down C Street not long after Andrew met Bobby's mother. Not to his real home yet, of course. He would still need a month or two of rehab for the leg at the Veterans' Hospital in Boston. But he's definitely home from St. Vincent's in New York so now he could be visited more often by his relatives and friends in Southie.

Marie was the first friend to visit him. She was accompanied by Mary and Jim who decided on a small wedding in the rectory of St. Brigid's. Jim wanted Bobby to be his best man.

"I'd be honored, Uncle Jim, provided I can walk." Marie explained that Andrew was taking a police exam that day. Then she asked Bobby if he would be Andrew's best man. "I dunno. I'm not sure, Marie. After what—"

"After what?" asked his mother.

"Nothing, Mom. It's just that...," he said as he averted her eyes, his voice trailing off.

Mary went no further but she privately vowed to get to the bottom of why Bobby's best friend, it seemed, might not be his best man. When Marie told Andrew about Bobby Mo's ambivalent answer, he told her to wait a little while.

"I'll get him to come around when he comes home. He's feeling a little lonely now. His whole life hinged on the thought that you loved him and he was going to live happily ever after with you."

"I did love him, I do love him. Only not in the way I love you."

"Really? Come over here. Show me the way you love me!"

"Get your hands off me, you beast! Let's talk about the wedding."

They had set the date for Saturday, June 8, 1946. It was to be held at St. Brigid's with the reception at the Veterans' Hall.

*****

Bobby Mo finally made it home, back to Southie, limping and aided by a cane. "They think I can throw this thing away in a year or so," he told anyone who asked.

When the weather was warm, he walked up and down the hilly streets of Southie as much as he could. Little kids would look at him limping and say, "Hey, mister! Were you in the war?"

"How'ja get that?" They pointed at the brace on his leg.

"Some bad guys did it."

"Who?" they asked, "Hitler?"

"Yeah, Hitler."

*****

Andrew, who was suffering from boredom while he waited word on his police application, ran into Bobby Mo one morning on East Broadway. It wasn't the first time they had seen each other since they came back but it was the first time they were together alone. Andrew pointed to a bench where they sat down in the bright morning South Boston sunshine.

"Thanks for what you did for me at St. Vith, Sarge. I think I would have—"

"No, you wouldn't, Bobby. It was a bad wound, I'll give you that. I did not save your life but you saved mine at Dix. You really saved my life from that nut, Chesterfield." They both laughed and remembered the times they had shared together. They hoped that Richard Chesterfield would turn out okay. "Bobby Mo, here's what I'd like to know. I never had a chance to ask you." Sarge was looking squarely into Bobby's eyes. "What motivated you to take off after that machine gun nest so quickly? Man! You just spotted it and ran toward them. Lucky you had two grenades. I froze when I saw the first one bounce back."

98

"Yeh, Sarge, I was lucky…until that sniper got me. Did they ever get him?"

"Yeah, a couple of our guys spotted him."

"Sarge, I don't know. I wasn't scared, I wasn't anything. Somehow I knew I was supposed to do something and I did it." He paused. "Maybe you thought that way at Guadalcanal."

"Maybe. I—" Sarge's attempt to remember what motivated him that day was cut off by Bobby.

"And maybe you spotted an opportunity with Marie and just went after it." Bobby Mo knew he never should have uttered that vile sentence, but it had been stored up in him for a long time. He looked at Sarge's stricken face. "I'm sorry, Sarge. I'm sorry. I'm just hurting a lot." Then he abruptly added, "Sarge, I really am sorry. There I am complaining and you just lost your father. Tell me, what was he like? We knew back at Dix that something was wrong when you left us for a few days. So what kind of father was he?"

Sarge was reeling from Bobby's third grenade but he managed to pull himself back. "He…he was a good guy in a lot of ways and not so good in others." Then the former Sgt. Andrew Vitkus who had always been extremely reticent about sharing his personal life with his subordinates poured it all out on the stunned Bobby Mo. "My mother didn't die in an accident, Bobby. She was raped and murdered."

He recounted the argument in the trailer that caused him to storm out that mid-September day in 1941 and described how he left Pawtucket and hitchhiked to Boston. But he left it there, never mentioning the Red Sox game. Then he told Bobby he joined the army as soon as he could. He skimmed over his exploits in the South Pacific and got quickly back to his father. It was as if he was living it all over again. He told Bobby about the deep sense of loss he felt when his father died. He cried a lot there on the bench as passersby glanced quizzically at them.

Bobby listened with his head down, not interrupting Sarge's soliloquy. When it ended, Bobby placed his right hand on Andrew's left shoulder. "I'm sorry, Sarge. It must have been really hard for you to lose your father like that just when you guys had it going."

It was time to leave. Sarge took advantage of the moment. "Bobby, this is Thursday. Why don't we get together on Saturday morning down at the new place, Sullivan's, out by the Castle. You, me, and Marie."

"Maybe, Sarge. Call me. No, have Marie call me."

They hugged briefly once more and headed off in different directions. Sarge hadn't gone far when he was stopped in his tracks by a sudden, terrifying thought. He had just poured out to Bobby Mo the pain he was experiencing at the death of his own father and Bobby had sympathized with him. Yet not once had he, Andrew Vitkus, empathized with Bobby about the sudden death of his father five years ago. Not once, in all these years, had he the common decency to say anything to a young man whose father had been suddenly taken from him. There were those secret reasons, yes, but still somehow.... As he walked away, the thought of what he had done five years ago, compounded by his sudden recognition of his own insensitivity concerning the hurt it had caused in Bobby, suddenly struck Andrew all over again. It terrified him. It erupted like a volcano that suddenly spews hot ash and lava and covered him all over. He turned to go back, Bobby Mo was out of sight.

Marie called Bobby Mo later that day. He said he would meet with her and Andrew on Saturday at 10:00 a.m.

*****

"Why'd we hafta meet here, out in the open? We could have met anywhere, why here?" Bobby Mo sat uncomfortably at the end of an old iron-and-wood bench. He turned halfway toward Marie and Sarge, his right arm awkwardly trying to grasp the top railing. He gave up finally and his arm flopped back on his lap. "Why?" Now he was alternately staring down at the pavement on which his feet nervously tapped and out toward the ocean. But never directly at Sarge and Marie.

The day had started ominously with heavy clouds pushed by an east wind off the ocean. The clouds had disappeared by the mid-morning and the wind softened into a gentle breeze. It was going to be a nice first Saturday in April in the year 1946 in South Boston, Massachusetts. Fifty yards away, Sullivan's had opened for the day and a line of thirty to forty eager children and adults had already formed for ice cream, hot dogs, and fried clams. Above the three of them, a quarter of a mile away on a hill overlooking Boston Harbor loomed Fort Independence, a huge granite edifice built in the early seventeenth century on what was then Castle Island but now was a stubby peninsula stuck on the end of that part of Boston known as South Boston.

"Bobby Mo," Marie turned fully toward him, trying to engage his eyes. She could not. But she persevered. She tried to give Bobby Mo a good answer as to why she had selected this place to meet. "Bobby, you know how you like it here near the water, looking up at the Fort. You used to come here as a kid a lot. Now there's Sullivan's. I know it wasn't here when you left, but I hear it's really good. Isn't that so, Sarge?" Former Sgt. Andrew Vitkus was not about to help the conversation along at that point so he merely nodded. But Marie, the girl with the straightforward approach to most everything in life, wouldn't let Bobby easily decline Sarge's request. "You two have been together now for almost three years. Bobby, you saved Sarge's life then he saved yours." She ignored Sarge's protests that he hadn't. "You've gone through things together that most men will never experience in their whole lives. He has asked you to do this. Actually,"—she threw a know-it-all look at Sarge—"he has no one else. Please say yes. It's so important to Sarge…and to me."

"*To you?* It means so much to *you?*" His voice turned low and dripped with sarcasm. Anger was welling up in Bobby Mo again. Like on the cold march to St. Vith when a fellow soldier inadvertently broke the news to him that he had been betrayed by his girlfriend and by his sergeant whose life he had once saved. Over the past few months, he had begun to wonder whether the sudden bravery he had exhibited in St. Vith was really a suicide rush. He exploded, "Are you both crazy? Be the best man for the guy who literally stole my girlfriend? I was gonna propose to you, Marie, when I got home. Right from under my eyes." He was sobbing as he spoke. "I don't think I'll ever be able to forgive you…both of you."

Marie was crying now. She tried to place her soft hand on Bobby's arm to calm him down. He pushed it off and pulled his arm away. "Bobby, Bobby Mo, we love you so much! Both of us! You know I love you, but I love Andrew too…in a different way. We couldn't help it, we just fell in love."

"That's great!" Bobby Mo was heaving convulsively now, trying to stop the tears. "That's great! But where does that leave me? I'm just supposed to be your best man, Sarge, and say, 'Have a happy honeymoon. And then you can have my kids. *My* kids, Sarge!" No one spoke for a few minutes. Neither Andrew nor Marie dared to touch Bobby, fearing he might explode once more. Then Bobby Mo looked up and nodded toward the long line at Sullivan's. Something…someone caught his eye. "I know what I'll do. I'll just have to find another girl to replace you, Marie. Maybe that one at the end of the line, that little blonde. She looks like she's alone. I'll go over there and ask her to marry me. Then maybe we can have a double wedding and we can be each other's best man, Sarge. Whaddya say?" Sarge stood up. He had *had* enough.

Marie spoke up. "Stop it, Bobby! Stop it!" Her left hand now tried to grip his arm.

He pulled it back. He made a feeble attempt to stand. He fell back, took a deep breath, and then forced himself to stand. He began to limp shakily away from Marie and Sarge and toward the end of the line. He looked back at them, rubbing his left forearm against his swollen eyes. Bobby Mo had no real intention of talking to the girl at the end of the line. He had no experience in the art of picking up girls. Marie had been his one and only girlfriend. Already the little blonde had been supplanted at the end of the line by a family of five.

"Hi, would you mind? She's a friend of mine."

They laughed and made way for him.

CHAPTER 19

S HE SPOKE BEFORE HE HAD a chance to say anything. Bobby Mo wasn't ready to say anything anyway. "This seems like a nice place. My roommate told me about it. She's going to meet me here. But it smells so good. And I'm hungry. So I'm in line," she said. "Are you, OK? You're not crying, are you? You're rubbing your eyes. What's good?"

"No, I have a bad cold. The fried clams, I think. I'm not sure. I just got out of the army a few weeks ago. This place is new, wasn't here when I left. My friends tell me that the food is great."

"I'm Ellen, Ellen Carlson. I'm new to Boston. New to the East. I'm from Zanesville, Ohio. Ever heard of it? Bet you haven't. I'm a freshman at Boston University (BU). I'm studying to be a nurse. How about you?"

"I'm Robert Mohegan. Most of my friends call me Bobby Mo. I don't know what I'm going to do yet. Maybe go to work for the Boston Edison, that's the electric company here in Boston."

"The Electric Company, Thomas Edison, Boston Edison. There's a connection there somewhere."

Bobby Mo laughed for the first time in that day. He looked at her. Blue eyes, blonde hair, and small but not too tiny alongside his six foot frame. The line for ice cream dwindled quickly. Inside, they were served by a horde of high school boys and girls behind the counter. He ordered for them both. Two large fried clams ("What are those ugly things?"), two frappes, ("What does *frappe* mean?"), and hot dogs ("I know what they are, all right."). He said he'd explain what a frappe was when they got outside.

"What's the matter with your leg, Bobby?"

"In Belgium, I got shot." He wasn't sure she believed him. "Honest, I got shot, Ellen. I'll tell you about it sometime."

"Sometime? How do you know there's gonna be a sometime?" He smiled at her in a way that said there would be. They stepped outside in the bright sunshine. Ellen's eyes sought a bench; Bobby's eyes sought Marie and Sarge. They were gone. He and Ellen found a bench. "You were crying, weren't you? I saw you look back. Were you with someone? I'll bet it was a girl. I'm sorry, I have no right to ask you those questions. I don't even know you, Bobby Mo…Bobby Mo what?"

"Yeah, Bobby Mohegan. Bobby Mo. C'mon, let's sit down for a minute so I can see if you like fried clams and a frappe. A frappe…I don't know where the name came from. All I know is that it's unique to Boston. I found all that out in the army. All it is, is a milkshake with ice cream. Don't roll your eyes like that. This is pure Boston stuff I'm telling you." Bobby tried to be serious, but their eyes locked and they laughed until they couldn't laugh anymore. Now they both were wiping the tears in their eyes with the back of their hands. After a while, Bobby admitted, "You were right, I was crying, for real about a girl. She was there with the guy she's gonna marry. It was supposed to be me."

"The three of you were there? On purpose or did you just run into each other?"

"On purpose. It was Marie's idea. She's the girl I wanted to marry. The guy's name is Andrew, Andrew Vitkus. We call him Sarge. He was actually my sergeant in the army. We became good friends. I saved his life once here in the States and he saved mine in Belgium when I got wounded. Don't look at me like that. It's true. I'll tell you sometime—"

"*Sometime*? But why were the three of you here today?"

"Ellen, I know this sounds crazy, but they're getting married in two months"—his voice rose as he spoke—"in the same church where I had planned to get married to her."

Ellen had suddenly become distracted. "There's Greta, my roommate. She's coming toward us. Hold it, Bobby. I'm going to run to her and see if I can hold her off for a few minutes." She jumped up and ran toward a waving Greta. Bobby watched as the two women talked out of earshot. Then Greta waved hello in his direction and headed toward the end of the food line. Ellen plopped back on the bench, a little out of breath, "I told her about the frappes. She'll be a few minutes. So what was the reason for the meeting?"

Bobby thought, *At least she's a good listener. She wants to hear the end of my story.* He waited a minute while she caught her breath. *God, she's pretty!* he thought. "They, both of them, want me to be his best man. Imagine, he not only steals my girlfriend, now I'm supposed to be the best man at the wedding."

"Bobby, there must be a reason. They both must like you a lot...."

Greta had disappeared into Sullivan's. Bobby knew that the conversation would turn mundane as soon as Greta joined them. His heart began to beat faster as if he knew he was going to lose a precious opportunity. What opportunity? He didn't know.

"I'd like to see you again, Ellen. Just to talk. I know it's only been—"

"Me too, Bobby." She smiled, and his heart raced even more.

"How about here next Saturday? Same time? Around ten."

"Ten, it is," she said, placing her hand on his ever so lightly.

"But what happens?" he said, anxiously now. "What happens if one of us can't make it? My mother doesn't have a phone. I saw a movie once about something like this. Cary Grant and Katherine Hepburn planned to meet and she got hit by a car and never made it. It was so sad."

"Then, big guy," she said with an impish smile, "then we'll never ever see each other again. How tragic."

My god! Bobby thought. *This woman has got it all!*

"Here comes Greta. Here's the number for my dorm. Call me there if you can't make it." Bobby and Ellen had stood up when Greta arrived. "Greta, this is Bobby Mohegan. You know, like *The Last of the Mohicans.* Only he's Irish, I think."

"Yes, Irish. Nice to meet you, Greta. Is she always as fresh as this?"

"Bobby, how are you going to get back home with your leg?" Greta now noticed Bobby's obvious discomfort.

"My Uncle Jim drove me down and he'll drive me back. As a matter of fact, he's been sitting over there in that green Chevy, waiting patiently for me for the last half hour. Good man, Uncle Jim."

Ellen looked up at Bobby. "Be sure to call me if you can't make it." She added, this time even more impishly, "Or if you don't want to see me again," Then she planted a kiss smack on his lips. "Bye, see you next Saturday at eleven."

The kiss was so sudden that he didn't have time to even give her an embrace in return. "Ten!" was all he could say.

"I know, I just wanted to make sure you got it straight. Bye!"

And with her blonde hair swishing back and forth, she was off.

*****

As they drove back up the hill, Uncle Jim spoke first. "Who was that lass, Bobby? I was watching the two of ye talking. She's pretty. What's her name?"

"Ellen, Uncle Jim. Ellen Carlson. She's from the Midwest. Goes to BU."

"Oh my god, that's a Protestant name, Bobby. And BU? That's a Protestant school. Ye had better not tell yer mother yet. At least, not right away. And what about Marie?"

"Marie's gone, Uncle Jim. You know that. Ellen's only someone I had a nice conversation with over fried clams."

That nice conversation ended with a nice kiss smack on the lips, thought Uncle Jim, but he said nothing more.

It was all so weird for Bobby that week. Without warning, he had gone almost simultaneously, from being an angry, jealous, and rejected suitor of a woman whose physical beauty and ebullient personality had bewitched him all the way through high school to becoming suddenly enamored by another woman he knew absolutely nothing about and who he would not be able to positively pick out from a chorus line of small, blonde Scandinavian women.

He laid in bed at night and tried to imagine Ellen's face in his mind. He couldn't.

On his walks up and down the hills of South Boston that week to gain strength in his left leg, he tried to picture her. No luck. "My god," he said to himself over and over again. "Is this some kind of fantasy I've created to keep me from coming unglued?" And then he began to worry that his second meeting might be washed away by a nor'easter on Saturday. He watched the news each night on all three channels and all three predicted heavy rains over the weekend. On his morning walk on Wednesday, he ran into Sarge who was excited about the news that he had been accepted by Boston as a Police Officer. He would begin his two-week training session next week and be on the street a month or so prior to the wedding.

"And I've got news for you, Sarge. If you'll have me after my sorry performance on Saturday, I'll be honored to be your best man."

Bobby didn't explain why he had changed his mind and Sarge didn't tell Bobby that he ran into Uncle Jim at Mass on Sunday. But Andrew couldn't resist a subtle rejoinder. "And who knows, Bobby, maybe one day, like you said last Saturday, I can be yours…if you'll have me."

*****

Andrew had Ellen's dorm telephone number. Based on the forecast, he thought it would be wise if he called her and called it off. That would not be an easy task. His mom had no phone. The only person he knew who had one was Marie's father, which would be awkward. So he held off. Bobby Mo went to bed early Friday night, hoping the forecasters were wrong.

Uncle Jim promised him a ride down to Sullivan's right after the eight thirty Saturday morning Mass at St. Brigid's with his bride-to-be. "And I should be able to drop yer mother off and pick ye up in time to get ye there at ten. I know ye haven't told her yet or I'd be hearing about it for sure by now."

"No, and don't you tell her either!"

All night long, the windows rattled and the roof groaned as the nor'easter struck. The rain hit South Boston horizontally during the early morning darkness before dawn. Bobby and his mother piled into Uncle Jim's Chevy at 8:00 a.m. Bobby tried his best to shield his mother from the rain but they both got soaked.

"What are ye up to, Bobby, that ye'd have to go out in this awful rain?"

"To go with you to Mass, Mom."

"I meant, after." She received no answer.

It was Bobby's first Mass since the day before St. Vith. That time, he wondered if it was to be his last. He also wondered whether Ellen would somehow be able to keep the date.

After Mass, Uncle Jim, the only one in the car who had a watch, looked over his shoulder at a soaking wet Bobby and said, "I've no time to take yer mom home first and then come back at ten."

"Come back at ten, what fer?"

"OK, Uncle Jim. Let's go right there."

"Right there?"

"To Sullivan's, Mom. To meet a girl."

"To meet a girl? What girl?"

Sullivan's was deserted. That is, except for a single taxi, a Checker. Its exhaust and fogged up windows gave away the fact that its engine was running.

"That's her! Thanks, Uncle Jim. I owe you one," said Bobby Mohegan as he pushed open the door against the violent wind. "Bye, Mom! Uncle Jim will explain!" As he limped across a hundred feet in the driving rain toward the taxi, Bobby laughed to himself. By the time they get home, Uncle Jim will have her convinced that Ellen is an Irish Catholic lass from Dorchester. He was crying and giddy as he limped the last few steps, sloshing through the puddles.

The rear window was being slowly cranked down and he heard her voice. "I thought you'd be early so I came early. Get in, you're soaked. Good heavens! Are you crying again? Are you going to cry every time we get together? This is Joe. I don't know your full name, Joe. Joe says there's a diner that's open over on Dot Ave, whatever that means…*Oh*, Dorchester Avenue! Thanks, Joe. He spotted it on the way here. We can go there and."

He shook off the water in his hair like a wet puppy. Then he brushed the wet hair off her face and held it firmly between his wet palms. "I want to look at you. I've been thinking all week that I might not recognize you. I—"

"I'm the only girl here."

"I know. I want to kiss you. I want to love you. I love you, it's crazy! I love you! Will you marry me? This is crazy! I can't say that, we don't even know each other. But I know it's right. You don't even know me. I feel like I've known you forever. Why?"

"I'm still the only girl here."

He couldn't laugh. He kissed her again and again as the cab pulled away in the driving rain and slowly made its way to the diner on Dot Ave. They spent the late morning and early afternoon at the diner. Joe said he had to go places but he promised to pick them up at four. Ellen was the most beautiful thing he had ever seen, he said. "*Thing?*" He laughed at everything she said. And he cried a lot.

That afternoon, Bobby Mo knew with certainty that something beyond human knowledge had happened to him at the back of the line at Sullivan's a week ago. As he *gazed*, for that is the proper word, into her eyes and as his eyes swept over her countenance time and again, he wondered if he could make her comprehend the depth of the love he felt for her at that moment. They talked easily all afternoon. Bobby Mo quickly ran through his life story, starting with his father's sudden and mysterious death five years ago. He explained that he had fallen in love with Marie as a freshman and thought she was in love enough to marry him and how she and Sarge had a similar experience as she and Bobby just had, but yet unknown to him as it was happening. As they sat there as the last customers in the diner, Bobby Mo had not thought through how his cataclysmic shift in prospective life partners would look to his mother who dearly loved Marie, to Marie's family, and even to Marie and Sarge. To anyone, really.

"So after Marie dumped you, you picked up this blonde right away at the end of the line at Sullivan's and you proposed to her the next Saturday and she said yes? She must be as crazy as you."

That's what he knew people would think. Maybe some, surely his mother, would say it to his face. Ellen's story was typical of a nice Protestant girl from Ohio who always delighted in taking care of people as a child, which, she explained, was why her career path led to nursing. Her mother and father were well-grounded members of a Congregational church back in Zanesville. She had a younger brother still in high school. She knew full well that her parents would be shocked at the thought of her falling in love so suddenly with an Irish Catholic boy from a place called South Boston and walked with a limp. She knew her mother would insist on a long period of prayer to be sure that what she was contemplating was the "will of God."

CHAPTER 20

*"Bobby! Bobby, me only son! And he wants to
marry a Protestant girl! Jesus, Mary, and Joseph,
what's this world coming to?"*

*"Marie, my beautiful daughter! Ye hardly
know this man who says he fell in love with yer
picture! And he's Polish! What's wrong with Bobby?
Why couldn't you find a nice Irish carpenter right
here in Southie?"*

*"And you're going to be married in a Protestant
church? Glory be to God, Bobby! Haven't I told ye
time and again never to set foot in one of them?"*

*"Marie, my god! I'll bet he doesn't even know
how to say a Hail Mary or an Our Father? Does he
even go to church?"*

I N SPITE OF ALL THE protestations from the Catholic and Protestant
parents, both wedding plans went forward. But in the hectic
interim, Sarge and Bobby Mo decided that they should visit
Manny Lopes in Walter Reed Hospital in Washington DC. So they
traveled by train to see him. On the six-hour trip, the two reminisced
about their time together. It was clear to both men that theirs was
to be a lifelong friendship. Andrew craftily steered their discussions
away from John Mohegan's death.

Manny was no longer in bed. He was sitting in a wheelchair,
tended to by a strikingly beautiful Spanish looking nurse. After emotional embraces, which confirmed the visitors' visual assumptions

that Manny had lost a lot off his once muscular frame, he introduced them to his nurse.

"Angelina, these are two of my best friends in the world. These are the guys I've told you so much about. This one here is Sgt. Andrew Vitkus and the other one is Bobby Mohegan. Some people call him Bobby Mo. I like 'Bobby' better. And this—stop staring at her, both of you—this is Angelina. She's been my nurse from the time I got here. She has got me up and walking with crutches. The doctors here have helped, of course." He laughed. "Anyway, when I met Angelina, her name was Nurse Angelina Restrepo Cardona and now it's Mrs. Angelina Cardona Lopes," he said proudly. Manny, the young soldier from Mexico via Southern California and Everett, Massachusetts, who had suffered a debilitating injury on a cold day in December 1944, in a little town in Belgium that few in America would ever know of, and had risked his life to back up a buddy in a firefight was now married to the gorgeous nurse who had helped him through his ordeal.

*****

South Boston was flooded with weddings in the spring of 1946 as dozens of veterans now in their mid-twenties, some of whom dedicated five years of their lives for their country, returned home. They were eager to recapture the time they had lost on the playing fields (they couldn't). They wanted to buy a brand new 1946 Ford or Chevy or Buick (they couldn't none were being made). They wanted to get married (there were plenty of nubile Irish lasses waiting for them) and wanted to have lots of kids (they eventually did).

The only hitch in Marie's and Andrew's wedding plans was when Tommy's name came up. Marie raised it. "Aren't you going to invite Tommy?"

"No."

"He's your brother."

"Half."

"We'll add him to the list. It's the right thing to do, Andrew. Maybe he won't come."

"He will, Marie. There'll be free food and good looking girls."

And so on Saturday, June 8, 1946, big Mike Callahan escorted his beloved Marie down the aisle of St. Brigid's Roman Catholic Church and handed her off to Police Officer Andrew Vitkus. Beside Andrew stood his best man, Robert Mohegan. The reception was held at the Veterans' Club on Front Street. Among the guests was a portly fellow wearing a modified zoot suit and showing off his date, a bosomy blonde in a shimmering, red, satin dress. He talked too loudly because he drank too much.

"You're doing great, big brother. Congratulations! And it looks like you're off to a great career as a cop. I hope nothing spoils it down the road."

"Nothing will, don't worry."

"I don't worry. Maybe it's you that has to."

A month later, Marie told Andrew she thought she was pregnant. Four months later, they were told to expect triplets.

*****

Because there was no Protestant Church in South Boston, Bobby Mo and Ellen Carlson's wedding took place on Saturday, August 10, 1946, in the First Baptist Church on Dot Avenue, not far from the diner where their first date took place during a nor'easter. Bobby Mo's bitter prediction on that fateful day at Sullivan's now seemed prescient. Andrew Vitkus was Bobby Mo's best man.

Although she had to pray at least ten rosaries and to beg Jesus and his holy mother to get her through the ordeal of entering a Protestant church, Mary Mohegan was there, escorted by her new husband, Jim. "I never would have married again but for the fact I didn't have to change me name. And glory be to God, Jim helped me through this ordeal." In the short time she had known Ellen Carlson, Mary Mohegan had come to the conclusion that she would be a good wife for Bobby. "And besides, I'm sure he'll have her converted in no time at all!" she said to herself. "Blessed be the name of Jesus."

The Callahans, who had been invited to the wedding at the behest of Marie, had other plans for the day. Their daughter Marie was not pleased.

CHAPTER 21

B Y THE YEAR 1950, ANDREW Vitkus, Bobby Mo, and Manny Lopes were the fathers and uncles of a combined number of seven children. Andrew and Marie led the way with triplets: Lucy, Lilly, and Lola on March 9, 1947. Bobby Mo and Ellen's were Irish twins born on May 2, 1947, and April 9, 1948, respectively.

"There's somethin' in the Mohegans' genes," Bobby Mo would say, citing the relationship between his dad and uncle Jim. The twins were appropriately named John and James.

Manny and Angelina adopted a boy and girl from Guatemala, six and four, named Fernand and Yilda. Andrew's fifty dollar weekly salary as a police officer was sufficient for him and Marie to find a three-bedroom flat on the second floor on Roanoke Avenue. Marie stayed home with "the trips," as she called them, worrying a lot about Andrew, who as a rookie police officer worked the midnight shift.

Bobby Mo and Ellen struggled at first. His bad leg gave him little prospect of finding meaningful work. Ellen stayed home with the kids. But her mother, imbued with the Midwestern work ethic, taught her daughter how to sew well. Ellen made a decent living for the family from home, designing and creating women's dresses. Because their income was sparse, Bobby Mo and Ellen accepted Mary's offer to live with her and Jim and share as much as possible in the expenses.

Manny and Angelina had also moved in with family, his extended one in Everett where accommodations were made for his handicap. Angelina continued working, this time as nurse in Boston City Hospital, to support Manny and their two children.

Andrew agreed to go to Sunday Mass regularly with Marie and the kids to bring them up in "the faith." Bobby Mo, much to his mother's chagrin often expressed in sniffling and pouting, made the decision to attend the little Protestant church on Dorchester Avenue on Sundays with Ellen and the kids and listen to the gospel preached by a timid young minister in a black suit, rather than attending St. Brigid's where a bombastic Catholic priest in a colorful chasuble and stole looked down at his parishioners from a raised pulpit every Sunday and asked for money to feed the poor.

All in all, though, the three young men had settled down with their wives and their young children to face the future. And each, although the circumstances through which they had met their wives were unusual, were still deeply in love with them.

*****

World War II had brought the three together as it did for millions of other men and women. Andrew, Bobby Mo, and Manny looked forward to a future where they, their wives, and their children, would be close friends *forever*.

By June 1950, when North Korea forces swept down on South Korea, Andrew Vitkus had been a police officer for four years. He found the work satisfying, if not particularly exciting. Even so, his evaluations were always outstanding. His "trips" were the love of his life. Each morning, he would arrive from work at the flat a little after eight and be greeted by three little three-year-old daughters in Mickey Mouse jammies singing with delight, "Daddy is home! Daddy is home!" Five nights a week, he would report to the South Boston Substation on the Boulevard at midnight. He decided to ignore his dying father's admonition that he must confess his crime sometime. Sometime maybe, but not now. He wouldn't allow himself to think about the irony of being a police officer and a forgotten killer.

At 12:30 a.m. on Monday, July 3, 1950, Andrew and his new partner, a rookie named Joey Napolitano, began their shift with a coffee and toast at Mal's Diner on Gurnet Street. They sat in a booth. Andrew's back was to the door. They were in uniform, of course. The only other customers were at the counter, two guys who seemed to lower their voices as the two police officers strode by. They left soon after.

"Sarge…" Andrew had picked up a following of fellow cops in his district who had heard about his exploits in the war and decided to let him keep the rank without portfolio. His partner lowered his voice. "Sarge, I know one of those guys. Bad guy from the North End. His name is Frankie, I don't know his last name. But I do know he's a furrier."

"A *furrier*?"

"Yeah, a guy who steals furs. I bet him and his buddy are casing some fur company around here. Look out the window, Sarge. They've got a big white van, perfect for furs. But now that they've seen us, they won't do anything tonight."

"I.J. Fox is over on Huntington Avenue, Joey. You're good. Let's see if I can get the shift commander to let us do a plainclothes gig tomorrow night."

And so it was that on the night of the Fourth of July in 1950, Police Officers Andrew Vitkus and Joey Napolitano, dressed in mufti, hardly paid attention to the brilliant fireworks exploding all over Boston while they watched with intense interest a large white van creep through the city streets and then, with its lights out, turn into the rear of a large brick building on Huntington Avenue marked I. J. Fox. The headlines in the early afternoon papers the next day and in the morning papers on July 6 told the story:

Hero Cop Does It Again

Silver Star winner stops major theft, robbers caught with a truckload of furs.

Police Officer Andrew Vitkus and his partner captured two men who had just robbed I.J. Fox Furriers, according to an I.J. Fox spokesman, of furs valued at approximately $100,000.

In spite of the fact that Andrew told the *Boston Post* reporter that is was Officer Joey Napolitano who was the source of the lead that led to the capture, he was not mentioned by name in the story. Despite Andrew's protestations to Joey and his fellow officers that he told the press about Joey's involvement, word got around that Andrew was a self-promoter. Andrew got a commendation and a promotion to sergeant. Joey just got a commendation. Now Andrew was Sarge for real again, this time with a bursting portfolio to back it up.

As the summer wore on, temperatures began to reach a hundred degrees in Boston. City Point Beach and Carson Beach in Southie became nighttime havens for thousands of men, women, and children who laid down on blankets or slouched on wooden benches or canvas beach chairs trying to get as much sleep as possible so they could deal with another day at work or a sweltering third-floor flat somewhere in the city.

A week or so after his latest exploit made the papers Andrew was handed the phone by Marie. "It's for you. I think it's your brother."

"Half brother...Hello?"

"Hi, big guy, it's Tommy. I seen in the paper that you're at it again. Good work. Dad would be real proud of you, he always was."

"Whaddya want, Tommy?"

"Andrew, listen, I'm in a little trouble. I need a few bucks is all, to clean it all up."

Andrew didn't want to know what "little trouble" Tommy was in. "How much?"

"Three hundred."

"Three hundred! Tommy, I only make fifty bucks a week for me, Marie, and three little kids to live on."

"It's only this one time."

"Yeah, I'll bet. OK, I'll talk to Marie and I'll get it to you. This one time only, right?"

Andrew knew there'd be another time. He was convinced that there would be more calls at other times and was now reasonably sure that Tommy had overhead him confess to his father that he had killed an innocent man in Boston a few years ago. He wondered if

Tommy clearly understood that the man he shot was Bobby Mo's father. "Of course he does," he said to himself. "He's just trying to figure out how to use what he knows to his own advantage."

*****

"Ellen tells me that Bobby gets melancholic this time of the year."

It was a lovely Saturday morning in early September. In the Vitkus household, Sarge was absorbed in trying to read the *Boston Globe* while fending off his four-year-old triplets who were climbing all over him, maliciously intent on keeping him from doing so. "Why so, Marie?" he said offhandedly.

"You know, his father's death. It's been nine years. His mother and Jim really have a hard time this time of year. Mary keeps wondering why they still haven't caught the guy. Do you think they ever will? Andrew, are you listening to me?"

"Yeah, Marie, I'm listening. I don't know the answer. It's been a long time." What else could Andrew say? How could he answer that question? Perhaps he could have been forthright. He could have said, "I hope not." And then responding to Marie's horrified, "What?" he could have answered, "Because all it would do would be to stir up raw emotions all over again." But he knew Marie would not accept that kind of answer so he lied. "I hope so," he said and prayed that his racing heart wouldn't cause him to snap at the kids, one of whom just put her finger up his nose.

"Take your finger out of Daddy's nose, Lucy!" Then Marie said, "Me too, Andrew. I hope they will eventually find him."

CHAPTER 22

THEN CAME THE NEWS THAT the Vitkuses and Mohegans hoped they would never hear but secretly thought they eventually would, Manny, Angelina, their adopted kids, and most of Manny's extended family were moving back to Southern California.

"It's too difficult for me up here in Boston in the winter. I can't move around much in the cold weather and I hate the snow and ice," Manny told Sarge and Bobby Mo one morning in a local coffee shop.

"Me too, Manny!" said Bobby Mo. "Can I go with you?"

Sarge, of course, cut in, "Will you ever shut up about the cold weather, Bobby! You did all right a few winters ago in St. Vith, didn't you? And didn't you tell me a week or so ago that you went ice skating, bad leg and all, with Ellen and the kids and loved it!" Then, without pausing, Sarge asked Manny, "What prompted it? Just the cold?"

"No, Sarge. Opportunity. My father and his brother, my uncle, still own 1,500 acres in Temecula, that's in Southern California. They want me to be the business manager for a new winery they want to develop there. And Angelina, she's a warm-weather girl. So…" A couple of tears rolled down his cheeks. So…I'm…we are going to miss you guys so much! But, Bobby Mo, think of where you can spend all your vacations, you and Ellen and the kids, in Southern California!"

Sarge and Bobby Mo blushed a little. Both of them would miss their dear friend whose wisdom and courage they cherished. As they were breaking up, Andrew watched as Bobby Mo limped toward the door. He quickly turned back to Manny who had to wait for a ride home to Everett. "Manny, I'll call you. I need to talk to you about something…important."

It was a spur-of-the-moment comment that Sarge made to Manny. He wasn't quite sure what prompted him to make it. For a week, he made no move to call him.

*****

Early on a cool September morning after a night of intense love-making, Andrew and Marie clung languorously to each other, awaiting the pounding of six little fists on their bedroom door, crying out, "Open up! Open up! It's us. Open up, Mommy. Open up, Daddy. We know you're in there"

The lovers knew they had maybe four minutes before the onslaught. Marie suddenly remembered something. "Oh yeah," she said. "I forgot to tell you. I was going to tell you before you got into bed. But then…"

"But then what?" Andrew kissed Marie's dreamy face again. "What were you going to tell me?"

"Well, remember I told you the other day how Mary Mohegan and Bobby get kind of upset this time of year?" Andrew suddenly pulled his head away from Marie's wet face. "Well, Mrs. Mohegan— Mary and Jim and even Bobby Mo all decided a couple of weeks ago that enough was enough. They wrote a letter to the police commissioner and had it signed by a lot of neighbors, asking for the case to be reopened. He just sent a letter back to Mary. Ellen read it to me over the phone. They're going to open the case up again. They said they would do their best to find poor Mr. Mohegan's killer. Finally! Isn't that great?"

Andrew pulled himself fully away Marie's warm body and sat up. "I think I hear the kids, they'll be coming soon. I better open the door for them. I'll make coffee. I'm hungry. You want breakfast?"

"Yes. But first, put some clothes on."

*****

For the past few months, Andrew began to have nightmares of hiding in the middle of the night in a swamp surrounded by swarms of howling bloodhounds and armed police officers waving flashlights and calling to him over loudspeakers to surrender or be killed. He would wake up, startled and terrified, and soaked with sweat. He would lie to Marie that it was a flashback to his days in the jungles of Guadalcanal. He knew the bad dreams were of the night eight years ago when he perched in terror on the muddy bank of a slow-moving stream under an arched bridge in the Fens near Fenway Park hoping his searchers wouldn't find him. That night, they were unsuccessful. Now they were going to be searching again. He was terrified at the thought of what could happen to him, to Marie, and to the three girls if they were successful. Reality began to set in, he needed someone to talk to. He decided to call Manny Lopes. They met at the same restaurant where the three of them had gotten together a few days ago. Andy made sure that Bobby Mo would be elsewhere during their meeting.

Manny walked in with difficulty, hampered by leg braces and crutches, accompanied by his seventeen-year-old nephew Joaquin who was his driver. He was promptly told by his uncle to "get lost" for a while. The waitress took their orders quickly and set hot coffee in front of them. As they sipped, Manny asked the obvious question, "So what's up, *amigo*? Is this supposed to be a secret meeting or something? No Bobby Mo?"

On the short drive across town that morning, Andrew Vitkus had prayed for the first time in his life. He had memorized prayers like the Our Father as a kid with his mother and occasionally said one out loud in a time of stress. This time, he spoke directly to God. "Oh God, if you exist, please help me today. Please help me tomorrow and in the future. Please don't let anything bad happen to Marie and the triplets. Please give me courage this morning and in the future to do the right thing." Now as he got ready to answer Manny's questions, he already had begun to lose courage. He tried to pull himself together to answer his question.

"Manny," he began, "you don't really know me. I'm not the man you think I am. Yeah,"—he held up his hand to ward off Manny's protest—"yeah, I'm OK in a lot of ways. But I'm not in a lot of others, Manny. I killed a guy nine years ago. Not in the army, not a Jap or a Nazi. No. I killed a man named John Mohegan. I killed Bobby Mohegan's father, I was the one who did it. I know that sounds crazy but it's true."

Manny leaned forward, looked intently at Andrew, and said, "Go ahead."

This time, there was no crying. Andrew Vitkus started with the argument he had with his father in the trailer, the accidental shooting, the resultant death of John Mohegan, the return to Pawtucket, running away to join the army, and the return to the States. But when he reached the part of his story about his shock at seeing Bobby Mohegan's name on the roster as he awaited his new recruits in September 1944, Manny held up his hand.

"Sarge, you're probably going to think this is crazy, but I'm not surprised. I'm not totally surprised."

"Wh-what are you talking about? How could you not be surprised? You didn't know. No one knew. No one knows…" His mind suddenly recalled that Tommy probably knew. "No one knew."

"Sarge, let me tell you. You remember the first night we showed up. You asked the corporal to read the roll?" Andrew didn't remember. "Then let me remind you. When you got to Bobby Mohegan's name, you stopped the corporal. You wanted to get a look at Bobby. I knew you did. I told Bobby the next day. Then you seemed to pay a lot of attention to him. On one of our runs, you asked about him. I knew you weren't hitting on him, I knew you liked girls. I always knew there was something there. I just couldn't put by finger on it. Whaddya going to do now? Now that you've told me, who else you gonna tell?"

Sarge suddenly become hungry. He ate his sandwich voraciously and gulped his black, very hot coffee. Then he sat back in the booth. Joaquin started to come over but Manny waved him off. "I dunno, Manny. What am I supposed to do? I'm a cop, a Boston cop. I'm a good cop, a real good cop. I like what I'm doing. If I confess, I'm done and I'll probably go to prison. Think of what Marie will say. What will she do? What will happen to her and our kids? How can I tell Bobby Mo, a guy I love? And Ellen and their kids? What a disgrace it will be to the families! Our three families love each other here in Southie." He paused. "Of course you're leaving us, you don't care anymore." He smiled, exhausted. "Manny, tell me what I should do…and don't tell me to confess. I could just resign from the police department. Never tell anyone. I know you won't rat me out. What should I do? I can't confess."

"Confess. Confess, Sarge. Confess to Bobby, to his mother, to Marie, to your superiors, and to everyone. Get it over with. It's been how long now, nine years? Confess!"

Andrew thought back to the conversations in the trailer with his father after Thanksgiving dinner. "Confess," his father said as Tommy pretended to be asleep.

Confession is not possible! So thought Patrol Sergeant Andrew Vitkus as he drove home from his meeting with Manny. He did admit to himself that he felt some relief now that he had revealed his secret to Manny. But to him, the imponderable consequences of a public confession were enough in this instance to thoroughly quash his innate desire to always be an openly honest man. Marie, for instance. He had won her over quickly. He had swept her off her feet that day in the parking lot in New York, but also by his intense desire to love her, to care for her, and to share his life with her. What would happen to their marriage if she were to find out? The kids? Bobby Mo? Bobby's mother? No. As much as he appreciated the advice given him by his dying father and by Manny, confession was not an option. He would have to somehow work his way through the rest of his life with that stain unwashed on his heart.

*****

Andrew liked working with the Joey Napolitano, the one who spotted and helped arrest the furriers on July 4th. That arrest had gotten Andrew promoted to sergeant. He had been assigned to the day shift to assist in training Joey. Andrew realized he was sleeping better and feeling better after his talk with Manny. Then, he suddenly saw the talk for what it was, a confession to Manny, just like his father had urged him to do. But he hadn't confessed to the extent his father and Manny had recommended. He knew his confession to Manny was made to salve his own conscience. There were no consequences to follow it. At least he told someone, just like he had told his father on that Thanksgiving night four years ago.

This morning, he and Joey were in a "roamer," a cruiser free to go anywhere in the city so Officer Napolitano could get a better idea of its geography. As they drove through Downtown Boston, Andrew bemoaned the fact that young recruits were quickly put on the street without any formal training. They finished their morning muffins and coffee at a shop on School Street near City Hall where Andrew regaled the kid with stories about Mayor James Michael Curley. They were about to reenter their cruiser when they heard what sounded like gunshots. Andrew turned on the new two-way Motorola radio and listened as the cruiser moved slowly off the curb.

Attention all units! Report of shots being fired in the vicinity of Prince Street. Report that the North End Savings Bank was just robbed! Two men, no description, ran away. A bank guard shot inside the bank. Attention all units!

"Let's go, kid. We're not far away!"

"But, Sarge, aren't we just a roamer?"

"A roamer with two good cops in it, kid." Andrew turned quickly to look at Joey. "You OK, kid? You OK? You look sick."

"I'm OK, Sarge. It's just that I ain't ever fired this thing," he said as he tapped his holstered .38 revolver.

"I thought they gave you young recruits at least some training. Well, they're gonna have to change the system somehow...soon!" he said to no one in particular as he moved cars and trucks magically out of his way with his howling siren and flashing blue lights. "OK, Joey, we're on Prince Street now. The dispatcher is saying that one of the creeps is running and he's got a gun. Believe it or not, he's coming our way...I think! I'm going to pull in here near this hydrant. Get out, kid, but stay behind your door. Got your gun out? Release the safety first. There you go. Try to stay low. Just don't get killed on your first month on the job. It wouldn't look good for the department and for me. I'm supposed to be looking out for you."

"Oh my god! Here he comes…and it looks like he's waiving a big .45! If you can, give me some cover. Look over the door once in a while."

Sarge stepped out, planted his feet, bent forward, and yelled with two hands on the .38, "Police! Police! Drop your gun! Drop it!"

The two were fifty feet apart now. The robber saw the cruiser, stopped running, twisted his short body halfway around, and aimed his gun at Sarge. He fired. The first bullet drilled into the car's radiator, setting off a hissing sound. He pulled his trigger twice more. Both shots hit the raised window on the passenger side door where Joey crouched in terror.

"Oh my god! Oh my god!" was all the kid could say.

Sarge did not fire his weapon. Instead, he ran toward the man who was suddenly distracted by the fact that his gun was jammed. Sarge hit him with his head and right shoulder smack in his gut. Upon impact, he staggered backward and then fell hard on the hot top. His gun flew out of his hand and bounced a couple of times. He hit his head hard. He was out cold!

Joey dared to look over the door in the few seconds of silence from behind the safety glass crumbling above his head. He saw it all. "Sarge! Sarge! Are you OK? Oh my god, Sarge! You were like Bronko Nagurski. The way you hit him and drove him back!"

Sarge was slowly rising to his feet, shaking off the pain from the back of his hands that had scraped the pavement under the robber's body. "Bronko who?"

"Bronko Nagurski. Never mind, Sarge. I guess you don't like football. Boy, he looks bad! I already called for an ambulance."

Residents of the three and six decker homes heard the shots and came out of their houses to find out what had happened.

Andrew was exhausted, breathing heavily. "I may need one too, I could use some oxygen. The guy probably got a fractured skull. He hit his head really hard. I had to tackle him. I couldn't shoot with all those people behind him. Could've hit someone!"

"Sarge." young Joey Napolitano, in spite of being untrained and terrified had mustered enough courage after the two shots that pierced the glass above him, to raise his head. He had seen it all: Sarge pointing his weapon at the robber. Sarge ordering him to drop his gun, but not firing his own weapon. Then furiously rushing him and slamming him to the pavement. "Sarge. I seen it all, Sarge. I seen it all. There wasn't nobody behind that guy. Nobody. The street was empty—you could have shot ten times and missed and still hit nobody, Sarge."

"No, kid! There were a lot of people behind him. I saw them! I didn't wanna shoot. I might have hit someone!"

Officer Napolitano heard something in the sergeant's tone and saw something in his eyes that told him to keep his mouth shut. Nevertheless, the next day when the papers came out with the story of the thwarted North End bank robbery, it again featured an account of how the decorated war hero, Sgt. Andrew Vitkus—this time, assisted by his rookie partner, Joe Napolitano—held his fire, even though he and his partner had been shot at, for fear of accidentally killing one of the neighborhood residents who were standing in shock behind the robber. Then he fearlessly tackled the man, to quote his partner, Officer Napolitano, "like Bronko Nagurski."

*****

"Daddy caught a bad guy, Mommy. Another one! He catches them all the time! The kids next door told us this morning!"

"Yes, girls, he does. But he's sleeping now, he needs to rest. And Mommy needs to be let alone for a few minutes while I make Daddy's lunch for when he wakes up."

When Sarge woke up, he didn't want to see the kids or talk to Marie right away. The previous day had been tiring with TV and newspaper reporters constantly in his face. Then there were reports to write. It had been difficult to get to sleep. He kept hashing the events of the previous day over and over again in his mind. Each scene was sharply in focus, except for the few seconds when he confronted the crazy bank robber firing at him and the rookie. He knew he had every right to return fire. He could have knocked the guy down easily from fifty feet with a few well-placed shots. He intended to return fire but he did not. Why? He reasoned, "If I had fired and missed, I might have killed an innocent person standing or walking behind the robber."

He laid in bed, trying to picture those persons. How many were they? Twenty? Ten? Five? Two? Only one? The kid said there were none. That couldn't be, he saw them. He could picture the robber again. Why couldn't he picture the innocent person he might have killed had he returned fire? His mind raced back nine years. Why hadn't he seen Bobby's father? He was much farther away. That was it. This time, the people were closer. But why couldn't he picture them now if they were so close yesterday? Maybe they were far off or maybe they weren't there. Maybe the kid was right. Maybe he could have shot and missed the robber ten times and not hit anyone because there was *no one there*! Which one was it? He did not know. He put his head deep into his pillow and pulled the covers over him. He wanted it all to go away. It did not.

*****

"Bobby's been getting a lot of strange calls lately."

"Really? From whom? About what?"

Marie was on her almost daily early morning telephone conversation with Ellen. "He says he's getting them two or three times a week at home and at Veterans Affairs from a weirdo."

"Really? By the way, how does he like his new job there? What's it about?"

"Loves his job. He's working on what they called punch cards. IBM. It helps with payroll. I—"

"No, I mean what are the calls about?"

"Believe it or not, they're about the investigation into his dad's murder. The guy says he knows who did it."

"Who does he say?"

"He won't say, unless Bobby gives him money. Sounds like an awful man. I don't know how he found out where Bobby lives. He saw the story in the paper about starting up the investigation. How would he know where Bobby worked?"

"How much does he want? Money, I mean."

"He says if Bobby will give him $300, he'll tell him who murdered his dad. Bobby just hangs up on him."

It was a coincidence, of course, thought Marie, *that the guy was asking for $300.* Her husband had been asked several times recently by his half brother if he could borrow the exact same amount. Andrew talked to Marie about Tommy's repeated requests for loans. They agreed to scrape together $300 three times. Each time was to be the last. She was the one to agree to the loans. "After all, Andrew, he's your brother, your half brother. Maybe he'll pay it back eventually." But it was Andrew who finally said, "No more!" to an angry Tommy Vitkus.

"*Wow!* That's too bad, Ellen," said Marie on the phone. "You guys don't have that much. The guy is just a scammer. How's the investigation going?"

"Just getting started, Marie. I don't think they'll ever find out, do you?"

"Don't know, but let's pray they do. Andrew is ambivalent. He thinks it will just stir up old memories. He's really tense these days. I can feel it and see it with me and the kids."

And so these two unlikely girlfriends joined their hearts in a long prayer that ended in, "And we ask all these things in Jesus's name."

CHAPTER 23

A LL DAY MARIE THOUGHT ABOUT the coincidence involving the $300. She almost called Ellen back to talk to her about the possibility of finding out if the caller was indeed Tommy. But what would he know about the murder of John Mohegan?

At supper that night while the kids watched TV, Andrew matter-of-factly told her about two events of the day. "There's a rumor that I may get promoted right up to lieutenant. All because of the bank job and the furs before that and because I won a Silver Star. Now there's talk they want me to be on the team to find Mr. Mohegan's killer. Honestly, Marie, I don't want to move too fast up the chain of command. Guys get jealous and I'm too close to Bobby Mo. Too close."

"I'm so glad you fell in love with me. You're such a good man, Andrew, to think that way. I love you dearly."

Andrew knew the caller had to be Tommy. Sooner or later—maybe sooner rather than later—he would give up Andrew's name. *That lousy bastard!* "Marie, why don't you call your mom and dad and ask them if they'll take the three little angels until ten while we sneak off down to the Point by the ocean and maybe even make out a little."

"We have a bed in the other room for that."

Andrew's heart was pounding. He knew his time was running out. If it wasn't going to be Tommy, it would be someone else or something else. "C'mon, will ya? I've got something I want to talk to you about."

"I'm not leaving Southie."

"You will if I say so." He laughed.

"Really?"

"Not really. Call your mom."

The triplets were in the custody of their adoring grandparents who warned them to be back by ten. "Because we are too old to do the bathtub thing and the putting-cryin'-kids-to-bed thing or to go through the 'We miss our mommy and daddy and want to go home right now' thing."

Andrew and Marie drove down to Sullivan's first for Cokes and ice cream and then drove back a quarter mile to City Point overlooking the harbor. It was a beautiful, warm night. The car windows were down and a soft breeze floated in from the ocean. Andrew pulled Marie close and kissed his wife passionlessly.

"Okay, big boy, what's up? I'd never have married you if I knew you kissed like that!"

Andrew discreetly pulled himself away from Marie until has back was against the driver's side door. He wanted to be looking directly at his wife when he at last revealed his secret. "Marie, I know this is going to be a shock to you. It's going to be the biggest shock of your life. It's going to be a shock to our marriage. It may not last because of what I'm going to tell you…"

Marie's body was suddenly consumed by an adrenaline rush, the kind she'd never before experienced. She couldn't think, she couldn't talk as she tried to catch her breath. *Did Andrew just say our marriage may not last? He's found someone else! Already?* Her thoughts screamed at her. While Andrew was trying to explain, he might just as well have been talking Hindi or Russian. She couldn't hear beyond "Our marriage may not last." She tried to pull herself together, clasping her breasts and trying to breathe. Finally, she was able to speak. "Is it another woman, Andrew? I can't believe it's another woman! I'd rather you said you killed someone than tell me you been cheating on me. I love you so much, Andrew. So, so much!" Marie's sobbing became convulsive. "How could it be? How could it be?"

Suddenly, she realized that Andrew had stopped speaking a foreign language. He broke through her hysteria. "It's *not* a woman, Marie. I will love you forever. I will always be faithful to you."

"Oh, thank God, Andrew! Oh thank God!"

"I did kill a man."

"I know you did, Andrew. Are you having flashbacks?" She was trying to control herself now.

"I am, Marie. I've had them for long time."

"Oh, Andrew. I feel so bad for you. That must have been horrible to remember those poor Japanese soldiers—"

"The man I killed was John Mohegan." He repeated it. "The man I killed a long time ago was John Mohegan. I killed Bobby's father, Marie. A long time ago!"

"But you didn't even know Bobby when Mr. Mohegan was killed. You met him three years later at boot camp. You couldn't have!"

"Marie!" Andrew took her sweaty hands in his. "If you can stop crying, I'll tell you the whole story."

It took Andrew an hour to tell the whole story to Marie. She cried the whole time, interrupting him often to ask questions she hoped would convince Andrew that his story was some sort of fantasy brought on by recent events. *After all,* she reasoned as she tried to take it all in, *how could Andrew have killed the father of his best friend?* It all seemed so much like a dream, except for the part about Andrew still being in love with her. That was real.

The sun had long since set. Neither had a watch. When Andrew drove back to Sullivan's, it had closed. "What time does it close?" he asked a final customer.

"Ten o'clock."

"We're in trouble, Marie. We've still got some talking to do. I have to tell Bobby, I have to tell the commissioner, and I have to make sure you and the kids are gonna be all right, no matter what happens."

"Don't worry about me, baby." She was now snuggled against him as they drove back to her parents' house, expecting to be subject to whatever punishment Mr. and Mrs. Mike Callahan were going to impose on them for being so late. Instead, they were told by the proud grandparents that the triplets had fallen asleep in their jammies and would need to be picked up before 8:00 a.m. "When we get home," said Marie, looking up at her relieved husband, "do you think you can kiss me with a little more passion than you did at the Point?"

CHAPTER 24

THEY HAD THE NIGHT TO spend together alone, but neither could sleep. Andrew tried to make up for his failure at lovemaking in the car at the beach. But he failed miserably again in his own bed. He turned away from Marie and fixed his eyes on the ceiling. She didn't mind. She laid on her back as well.

Marie woke up angry from a fitful sleep. "Andrew, why didn't you deal with *that thing* a long time ago?"

"That thing" quickly had become a euphemism for "the killing" or "the murder."

"If you had, it would have been all over. You would have had to go to prison for a short time. It was an accident, after all. Then you would have been free. Why didn't you confess then? Now look at the mess we're in!" Marie's eyes were red from the rubbing.

Andrew tried to calm her down. "And then, my darling, I never would have met Bobby Mo, except maybe in a courtroom. I never would have met you and we wouldn't have those kids who we're going to pick up at your mother's house in an hour."

Later with the kids home and running around, Marie and Andrew sat looking out from their tiny porch toward the ocean and the rising sun over Boston Harbor. Marie was frightened, Andrew was not. He tried to assure her that everything would work out in the long run.

"Marie, remember what Father what's-his-name said at Mass on Sunday? I think it was from the book of Hebrews. I wrote it down. It went like this, 'The Lord is my helper. I will not be afraid. What will man do to me?'"

That was reassuring to Marie. First, because she believed it. And second, because she knew Andrew was listening and thinking about what he was hearing at Sunday Mass. So they began to plan how to proceed. First to hear the horrifying news would be Bobby Mo and Ellen. Maybe they'd let Bobby tell his mother and Jim, maybe they would not have to do it themselves. Next would be Marie's parents. That would be awful for Marie. Andrew told Marie that Manny already knew.

"That sounds like a good couple of first steps, honey," he said.

Marie asked, "Who comes next? After we've told all our relatives and friends? Who comes next?"

"Do you mean the police department? I've thought a lot about that. I kinda think I might postpone that for a while. What good will it do…I mean, for us?"

"What good will it do?" Andrew intended his question to be rhetorical, but Marie treated it as requiring an answer.

"This is what it would do, my dear husband. First, it would finally clear your conscience. Honey, it would wipe your slate clean. You've been carrying a heavy load for a long time. Maybe if you had never met Bobby—But he deserves to know. Oh, I know, I know! You're going to tell him and Ellen, his mother and Jim, and my mom and dad. But your conscience is always going to nag you about what you did until everyone who knows you—us—knows about it. You've got to tell the police department and the public. Everyone!"

"But, Marie, I—"

She wouldn't let him interrupt. "Andrew, I've been thinking about that bank robbery arrest. The papers said you didn't shoot the guy because you thought if you missed him, you might hit an innocent bystander. So you tackled him like…"

"Like Bronco somebody, the kid said. I didn't know who he was talking about."

"Andrew, tell me the truth. You could have shot him easily. He was shooting at you two guys! He could have killed you or the Napolitano kid and you didn't shoot back. I know it wasn't out of the goodness of your heart that you didn't shoot him. What were you afraid of? Were you thinking back to Mr. Mohegan?"

"I don't know. I saw people behind him but the kid said no one was there. Now I can't remember seeing anyone. I can't picture anyone. I *am* tired of all this, Marie. If I was single now, I think I'd just continue on and not tell a soul. But now I have you and the kids to worry about. I probably won't be a cop when *this thing* is all done. Maybe I'll have to serve some time—"

"Maybe! Maybe! Maybe! No more *maybes*! Let's get together with Bobby and Ellen soon. Let's get that over with soon. Maybe later today, even this afternoon."

*****

"Marie, can you grab the phone? I'm in the middle of shaving."

"Honey, Andrew, it's for you. A lieutenant from the Cranston Police Department. Says it's about Tommy. I hope he's all right. Cranston is in Rhode Island, right?"

"Yeah. Hi, yes, this is Lieutenant Vitkus." Pause. "Yes, he's my brother, half brother." Pause. "*Oh wow!*" Pause. "When?" Pause. "*Oh my!* Are you sure? Thanks, Lieutenant." He quickly told Marie. "*Oh my god*, Marie! Tommy's gone. I can't believe it! Dear God!"

"Gone? Tommy's gone? Gone where? *Oh my god!* Andrew, I'm so sorry!" Marie embraced her husband who had begun sobbing into his right arm against the kitchen wall.

"He really wasn't a bad guy, Marie. He had a rough upbringing. Always wanted to be a big shot, tried too hard. Hung with the wrong guys. They found him alongside route 1, shot three times. I'll have to make sure he has a proper funeral, I guess. I don't think he had anybody to speak of, really."

"Of course, Andrew, of course."

"How come Daddy's crying, Mommy?"

"Uncle Tommy died, sweetie."

"He did? *Wow!* Who's Uncle Tommy?"

The phone rang a second time. Marie answered with trepidation and listened for a while, hardly speaking. Then she handed the phone to her husband, "It's for you again, Andrew. Says he's a former cop. Says the bank robber you tackled was his nephew. He wants to thank you in person for not shooting him. Wants to come see you this afternoon."

This afternoon, Andrew thought. *That would mean postponing his talk with Bobby Mo.* "OK, tell him to come by after lunch."

*****

Marie had an afternoon shift at the hospital so Andrew had the triplets all to himself. They were in a foul mood after lunch.

"You don't make marshmallow and jelly sandwiches like Mommy."

"She spreads it neat. You're messy, Daddy."

"Why do we hafta clean up? Mommy always cleans up for us."

Andrew had just pronounced that last complaint a downright lie when the doorbell rang. He shoved the three girls in front of the TV to watch *I Love Lucy* reruns and greeted his visitor.

"I'm Edmund O'Brien."

"Hi, Mr. O'Brien. Come in. Want some tea and Irish bread? My wife just made the bread. She told me you were a retired cop and that you wanted to meet me in person. Marie, my wife, said the kid I grabbed the other day was your nephew and you wanted to thank me for not shooting him." Mr. O'Brien raised his right palm and tried to stop Andrew, but he continued anyway. "Too bad. Seems like he's gonna be in big trouble. Must be hard on your sister or brother. Has he been in trouble before?"

"Neither my brother or sister. I don't have any siblings so no nephews."

"I don't get it, Mr. O'Brien."

"I needed some sort of excuse to meet you again."

"Again, Mr. O'Brien? I'm not following you. We met somewhere else, did we? The army? No, you're a bit older than me."

The *I Love Lucy* rerun was over. The clever little triplets began to crawl warily back into the room in spread formation so their father wouldn't be able to issue his threatening stare at them as a unit. Soon Lucy was at Mr. O'Brien's feet, attempting unsuccessfully to tie the loose shoelace on his right foot. So interested in Mr. O'Brien's story was Andrew that he hardly noticed the skullduggery until the victim reached down to touch lightly on her head.

"Lucy!"

"No mind, sir. Mrs. O'Brien and me, we never had kids. Just one of those things. I don't mind."

"But where did we meet, Mr. O'Brien?"

The visitor took a different tack. "Like I said, Andrew—Can I call you that?"

"Of course."

"Like I said, I never had much excitement all my years as a cop. Not like you, young man. I've been reading about you in the papers for the last couple of months. First time, at the I.J. Fox robbery and the second, the other day. The bank robber...stupid idiot! Thank God he wasn't my nephew. You shoulda shot the little creep!"

"*Whoa*, Mr. O'Brien! *Whoa!* I'm not supposed to use my weapon unless it's absolutely necessary."

"*Wasn't* necessary? He was shooting at the two of you!" Mr. O'Brien's voice rose. "Seems to me it *was* necessary."

Where was this conversation going? Andrew was confused. "I could have hit an innocent bystander if I missed him, Mr. O'Brien. Girls! Why are you pulling at Mr. O'Brien's trousers? Excuse me, Mr. O'Brien. They're driving me crazy!" Andrew had enough. In one fell swoop, he grabbed the three of them and deposited their howling bodies back in front of the TV in their bedroom. "Where were we?" he said as he returned out of breath. "Oh yeah, your fake nephew." He was beginning to be irritated by Mr. O'Brien's manner and his crazy question.

Mr. O'Brien continued, "How would you have missed him? You were as close as Ted was to Passeau in the All-Star game."

"What?"

"Sixty feet. I can see you don't follow baseball. What were you afraid of?"

"Mr. O'Brien, I'm confused! What are you talking about? I've never seen you before. You come into my house and start demanding I tell you why I didn't shoot a guy. It's really not your business and it's really not a subject I'd like to talk about, if you don't mind." Andrew stood up. "Mr. O'Brien, I think it's about time you left."

Mr. O'Brien still sat. He wasn't going anywhere. "Mr. Vitkus. It really *is* my business. And I believe we *have* met before."

Andrew sat down. The kids were peeking in again, alerted by the rising voices. "Just what are you saying, Mr. O'Brien?"

"I'm saying, young man…I'm saying that you were the man who shot and killed an innocent man outside of Fenway Park in Boston on September 15, 1941. And I'm saying that I know all that because I was the cop you pulled the gun away from and then fired the shot that killed a man named John Mohegan. That's what I'm saying, that's what I'm saying." Mr. O'Brien's face contorted into a rubbery blob and his cheeks were covered with tears. "Do you think I like this, Mr. Vitkus? I've spent days and hours for the last nine years thinking about you, about meeting you face-to-face one day. There were many nights I couldn't sleep thinking about how or why I let you grab my gun and kill that man!"

"I don't know what you're talking about, Mr. O'Brien. I never killed anybody, except Japs. Not even Germans. Why would you accuse me of such a thing?" Andrew's panicked state of mind couldn't find a way to respond except with a bald-face lie. But his protests sounded weak. He settled back in his chair. He wanted to cry but dared not, lest his culpability be suddenly exposed.

"Daddy, we're bored! We want to come out here with you and Mr. O'Brien. You guys were talking real loud. Are you two mad at each other?"

Andrew stood up again to scold the girls. But Mr. O'Brien stopped him. "No, Andrew, let them come in. I don't mind. Mrs. O'Brien and me, we never had kids. Here—which one are you? Oh, Lucy. OK, come sit on my lap. Is that okay, Mr. Vitkus?"

"Absolutely, Mr. O'Brien. That's fine."

"He's not Mr. O'Brien, Daddy. He's Mr. O'Bee. We thought that up when you guys were fighting or something. Mr. O'Bee!"

"Girls!"

"No, that's OK, Mr. Vitkus. I kind of like that. Mr. O'Bee."

Both men had become temperate again. "Mr. O'Brien. Just suppose you're right for a moment—and I want you to know that—"

Mr. O'Brien waived him off. "Just suppose for a minute, OK? I hadn't thought as much about it for years since Mrs. O'Brien— Helen died. But then, I seen your picture in the paper—two times. And I said to myself… Who does Sergeant Vitkus look like to you? To me. And I thought a bit, and I say Sergeant Vitkus looks like that kid nine years ago. But that's impossible. This guy is a Cop—one of my own. Stop it! I say to myself. Then I read the story—the last one about the bank robber. And it quotes you—the story does—it says you were afraid of shooting the guy, you know, my 'nephew'." Both men grudgingly smiled at the weak attempt at humor. "Because you were afraid of hitting a bystander. But you could have drilled him easy from such a short distance and you didn't. You ran toward him, risking your own life and maybe your partner's, if the jerk could shoot good. You tackled him instead, your partner says, like Bronko…"

By this time, Andrew had heard from dozens of his friends about his lack of knowledge of Nagurski so he didn't say, "Bronko who?" He said, "Pretty weak, Mr. O'Brien. Pretty weak. How could you conclude that I was the guy who shot my best friend's father with all that supposing—suppose this and suppose that! Nobody would believe that story, Mr. O'Brien. Nobody."

"Maybe so, Andrew. That's how I felt too until I read the story about you winning the Silver Star out there somewhere…"

"At Guadalcanal"

"Right, at Guadalcanal. In that story, Andrew, it says that you grew up in Pawtucket, Rhode Island. Never been there myself."

"So what, Mr. O'Brien! So what!" Andrew's indignation was now real.

"You're right, Andrew. So what! I didn't pay no attention to it until a coupla weeks ago. The superintendent decided he wanted me to be on the new committee to find Mr. Mohegan's killer. I liked the idea. We've had only one meeting so far. A coupla weeks ago, like I said. At the meeting, they drag out this plastic bag from the evidence room. There was nothing much in there except a muddy sweatshirt that they found near the Muddy River they think could have been tossed aside by the kid as he ran away and probably hid somewhere near there that night." Andrew could hardly breathe. "And you know what it said on it, Andrew?" Andrew tried to say no but couldn't. "It said 'Pawtucket High School Track Team'."

"That's not enough evidence to convict anyone. You know that, Mr. O'Brien. You were a cop."

"Probably, Mr. Vitkus. Probably. But I do know it's plenty to embarrass anyone."

"Are you looking to threaten me, Mr. O'Brien? If you are, you had better leave right now!" Andrew stood up.

Mr. O'Brien could not. Lucy was on his lap, playing with his tie. "No, I'm not, Andrew. But remember, I'm on the committee to find you, find the killer. The stuff that I just told you has a way of being put together. The committee is bound to ask me a lot of questions about what the shooter"—he dropped the word *killer* earlier—"what he would look like and so forth. I'm going to be under a lot of pressure. Unless..."

"Unless?"

"Unless the shooter comes forward himself and confesses to what he did. Then I can say, 'I'm not sure. It's been a long time. How could I be expected to remember?'"

"I'm not sure, Mr. O'Brien? I'm *not sure?*"

"No, no, I'll probably say, 'He's not him. I'm sure that Officer Vitkus, he's not him. I'm sure.' That Irish bread all gone? I'd sure like another piece. How about you, Lucy? You want some of your Mommy's Irish bread?" Mr. O'Brien asked as he bent down to nuzzle her soft blonde hair.

*****

When Marie came home from her shift, Andrew told her about Mr. O'Brien's visit.

"*My god*, Marie, if he hadn't fallen in love with our bratty kids, I think we might have come to blows. Lucy, especially. She said his name was Mr. O'Bee. I could have conked her when she said that, but he loved it. It was really something to see. Poor guy. Really lonely."

"So what are you going to do now, Andrew?"

"Confess! My father told me. Manny told me. You've told me." Andrew knew then that the moment he had dreaded for nine years was now upon him. "Marie, call Ellen. Tell her we'd like to drop by after supper. Say it's kind of important."

The triplets were delighted at the prospect of a cookout at Uncle Bobby's and Aunt Ellen's house and the chance to play with their cousins, Jack and Jim. The three held hands and skipped ahead of their parents down the steep hill and over the two streets toward the Mohegans' house.

Andrew and Marie took the time offered them to talk about Bobby Mo's possible reaction to the dreadful news he was about to hear. Would he be shocked? Of course. Would he be angry? For sure. How would the news affect the deep friendship the two men had forged over the past six years? As the two walked along, they both remembered how Bobby had reacted when he heard the news on the ruck march in Belgium on that cold, snowy night six years ago.

"But he got over it then, Marie. I told you how he put aside his feelings toward me the very next day and took out that machine gun nest in St. Vith."

"Yeah, honey. But there were other factors that came into play then. Like war! And don't ever forget what he said when we asked him to be your best man down at Sullivan's. 'I'll never forgive you two,' he said."

"He did though, honey, didn't he?"

"Him meeting Ellen saved us that day," she said. "Thank God for Ellen."

It was a pleasant night. The smoke from John Mohegan's old charcoal grill filled the air pleasantly. Andrew was surprised to see Mary and Jim there. Jim was doing the cooking. Mary was sitting back on her and John's old battered chaise lounge, sipping a gin and tonic. The five kids were running in and out of the house, playing hide and seek.

They wondered then how Mary would react. And Jim? And the investigation. What would happen to that? Andrew wondered how he would handle the situation. He had often pictured himself confessing to Bobby Mo first, and then letting the news trickle out to the rest of the family. He knew that was a cowardly way but he didn't think he had the emotional energy to confess one by one to each of them. What if Bobby Mo went off on him, like he did down at Sullivan's? He milled around a bit, trying to get in position so he and Bobby Mo could sit off to the side and talk privately.

Marie, however, caught his movements out of the corner of her eye. She knew just what he was doing. *He's gonna tell Bobby off to the side. Then he's gonna try to get us to scoot out of here. Bobby will be left with the rest of them to tell, especially his mother. No way!* She stood up. "Hey, everyone! What a great night! Everyone having a good time? Andrew has something to tell you all. And we thought—"

"Marie, that's not the way—"

"A home run's better than four straight singles, that's what Bobby Mohegan told me in high school. I wasn't sure then what you were getting at, Bobby, but now I know. So, Andrew, hit a home run, honey." They all laughed, except Andrew. Marie issued a command. "Bobby, come over here. Sit next to Andrew and me. Mary and Jim and Ellen, please join us." No one spoke. They did what Marie told them to do.

Andrew's face, a little flushed from two beers, now showed obvious signs of stress. He tried to compose himself. "Bobby...Bobby Mo, you know how much I love you and Ellen and Jack and Jimmy. And you too, Mary and Jim. You know..." He began to cry softly. No one said a word. A cruise ship in the harbor made an eerie whistle. No one turned an ear to it. "Bobby, a long time ago, when I was an eighteen-year-old kid in Pawtucket...You know I lived in Pawtucket, Bobby?"

"Right, I did. I knew you lived in Pawtucket, Sarge."

"Well, anyway, it was September 1942. How old were you then, Bobby?"

"Fifteen, Sarge."

"I was eighteen. I wasn't getting along with my dad, my father."

"I know, Sarge."

Marie looked at Mary who was beginning to sob softly. Jim's face was impassive. Ellen had her head down and her hands were fidgeting in her lap.

"Bobby, I was so unbelievably hungry."

"Where *were* you, Sarge? That day?"

"Oh, up in Boston. Near Fenway Park."

"You never went to a baseball game in your life, Sarge."

"No, not at the game. I wasn't at the game."

"That was the game where my father got shot, wasn't it, Sarge?"

Andrew stopped. He was perplexed. Bobby seemed to anticipate everything he was trying to say. "Yes, that game, Bobby. Bobby, you know how much I love you." He looked now at Mary. "And I love you too, Mary."

"I know, Sarge, and I forgive you. So does my mom. Right, Mom? You forgive Andrew, don't you?" Mary nodded her head though tears.

Forgive me? Forgive me for what? Andrew's mind raced madly about. *Do they know I killed John Mohegan? How could they?* He looked now at Bobby Mo who seemed to be smiling as he listened to him. "Bobby, I...I..." He began to sob convulsively.

"Sarge, Sarge, listen to me. I know you were the one who fired the shot that accidentally hit my dad." Bobby couldn't bring himself to say, "killed my dad."

Andrew didn't comprehend what Bobby was saying. "Bobby! Bobby! I killed your dad that day! It was me, Bobby! It was me! I could never tell you. I hid it from you, from everyone. And then you come down to Dix and we became friends, sort of. And then, dammit, you saved my life! *Oh my god!* It's all so crazy. Bobby, will you forgive me? Can you ever forgive me?"

"Sarge, Sarge, calm down! I forgive you. I forgave you. Forgave, Sarge. Forgave. Past tense, Sarge. Past tense."

A sudden cold east wind blew in off the ocean. No one paid attention. Andrew began to realize some degree of comprehension as he looked up at Bobby Mo.

Bobby put up his hand. "Sarge, Stop! Stop it right now!"

Andrew sucked in the cool wind and began to get control of his emotions. "I don't understand, Bobby. How could you have found out?"

"It was Manny, Sarge. Not that he told me, I figured it out myself. I bumped into him one day on my walks on the hill and we talked for a long while. He seemed to be driving at something but I couldn't figure out what. He reminded me of that first day at Dix and the roll call and the way you always seemed to pay extra attention to Manny and me, mostly me."

"That's not much, Bobby."

"Right, Sarge. But then, believe it or not, word leaked out from the committee. Nobody can keep a secret, and Uncle Jim over there with his arm around my mom—"

"To keep her warm, Bobby. To keep her warm."

"Uncle Jim heard that the only evidence the committee had was a dirty old sweatshirt that the shooter had tossed aside. You know what it said on it, Sarge? It said 'Pawtucket High School Track Team.' Sarge, I remembered one day on one of those torturous runs you used to put us through at Dix that you had been a track star at Pawtucket High School. I did a lot of thinking. I still wasn't sure." Copious tears were streaming down Andrew's face. He paid no attention to them except to occasionally wipe them off with his forearm. As he sat there, his guilt fully exposed in front of the assembled jury of friends and loved ones, waiting to hear Bobby explain how he knew. "I wasn't sure, Sarge. It seemed unbelievable. So you know what I did then?"

"I think I can guess. Manny?"

"Right. All I wanted to do was to talk to him, to think it all through. I didn't want to believe I was right. And he listened to me, Sarge. All the way. Then I said, 'Manny, what do you think? Could it be true?' You know what he did, Sarge, what he said? He said you already confessed to him one day on the hill. When we were finished, before I could even get worked up, you know what he said, Sarge? Well, you already know what he would say, don't you, Sarge? Tell me what he told me I should do."

The wind had picked up. It rustled through the trees. No one noticed. The kids had gone inside. "I don't even have to guess, Bobby…" Sarge was having trouble talking at all so he spoke slowly. "I think…I think he must have told you to forgive me. Am I right, Bobby?"

"You're right, Sgt. Andrew Vitkus. That's what Manny told me that night on the phone a few days ago. So that's what I've been trying to get through to you all night. That I forgive you. Fully. Forever!"

"In the name of Jesus," Ellen said from the corner of the crowd.

"In the name of Jesus," Bobby Mo echoed.

"I forgive ye as well, Andrew. In case you'd like to know."

"Oh, Mary! Thank you."

"Me too, Andrew."

"Thanks, Jim. I appreciate that."

*****

Much later, Andrew had to admonish himself for wondering if the easy forgiveness coming from the widow and her new husband stemmed in part from their newfound deep love for each other. On their way home, Andrew and Marie had to take turns carrying the triplets who were dead tired from the almost inexhaustible fun of hanging out with their cousins. Andrew began to think about the steps he must take next.

"This week, I'll see the superintendent first then the commissioner. I want to go up the ladder, follow the chain of command, like the good soldier that I am…or was." He smiled wryly. "They'll want to know what I'm asking to see them for. I'll tell each of them that it's personal, and it sure will be, won't it? But they'll see me. The super is a great guy, a guy's guy. I'm not sure about the commissioner. I do know he's got bigger and better things on his mind. Mayor, maybe. Or Governor. Senator. Who knows? I'm not sure how he'll handle it."

"Andrew, you're…we're going to need a lawyer. You've got to protect yourself."

"Don't worry, honey. I've got a good one in mind. Good Irish kid. But I don't want to bring him in now. I want to do this first part myself."

Outwardly, Andrew sported confidence when he talked to Marie about the situation, but inwardly, he was terrified at the thought of what could happen to his family after he told the authorities what he had done on September 14, 1941.

*****

The next morning, he made his appointments, one at 10:00 a.m. with the superintendent and the other through Darlene, the commissioner's secretary, an hour later. The two men's offices were a floor apart. Andrew hoped they or their secretaries wouldn't figure out that Andrew had set up two separate meetings and would try to merge them.

As he was dressing that morning, Marie, half asleep, asked why he wasn't in uniform. "You know, honey. I know the super pretty well, he's a good guy. But the commissioner, I don't know. I'm a little afraid of what he might do when he hears my story. Suppose he says, 'Officer Vitkus, you're a disgrace to the Department. I want your badge and your gun now on the way out that door!'"

"He wouldn't do that, honey. That would be awful."

"It would be, wouldn't it? But he can't do it if I go in there on leave for a day. I don't have my gun or my badge with me. I'll wear a nice white shirt and tie. No uniform. Just to be sure."

"Andrew, honey," Marie was out of bed. She ran to him, her tiny bare feet hardly making a sound on the wood floor. She threw her arms around his half naked body and clung to him. "Andrew, you must be so nervous, honey. Are you?"

"Nervous as a cat."

"Then we have to pray. Ellen and Bobby pray together every day. She says Jesus always answers their prayers. We don't pray as much."

"Whatta we gonna pray for, baby? That I won't be fired? That I'll even get promoted today?"

"Andrew, stop it. Let's ask Jesus before you go that good things will come out of today's meetings. God only knows."

"All right, but not until you put some clothes on. I can't pray with you in that nightgown through which I can see everything!"

*****

The superintendent was happy to see Andrew. He was blessed with an ebullient personality that allowed visitors to get their point or points across early and easily. He congratulated the sergeant on all he was doing out there on the street. "Sergeant, that arrest you made last week was outstanding. The commissioner was ecstatic. I think you must have heard the rumors. You're going to be a lieutenant, the youngest one ever."

It was Andrew's chance. "I don't think so, sir. I—"

"And we'll set up a nice ceremony. I—What did you say, Sergeant? *You don't think so?*"

So Andrew began telling his astonished superior the long-hidden story of the unsolved murder of John Mohegan nine years ago. He had told it so many times recently that now it came off as a dispassionate recounting of a story about someone else, not him.

"*Oh my god! Oh my god!* I can't believe this, Andrew! Is this true? Are you making this all up somehow?" The superintendent began to cry. Andrew sat passively. He had cried each other time he confessed, not this time. "Sergeant! Andrew! I've got to tell the commissioner about this right away! He'll go crazy. No telling what he'll do."

"Sir, I'm going up to see him right now. I mean, after this, I kind of hoped you'd go up with me. I made an appointment with him yesterday."

"Of course, Andrew. Of course. I...give me a couple of minutes. I don't want him to see me like this."

"Sure, sir. I've cried a lot of times about this. I understand."

"Of course. Say, does the Mohegan family know? I mean, about you? I mean, about young Mohegan's father?"

"Bobby does, sir. I told him just a few days ago. He said he actually forgave me. Can you believe it? He forgave me? He's my best

WHAT DID TED HAVE?

friend, still is. We went through some tough times. He saved my life once here in the States. He..." The superintendent wasn't listening. He was preparing himself to go upstairs.

The commissioner was a handsome and gruff man who reserved his smiles for the camera. He sat behind a huge, intricately carved, dark walnut desk that Andrew guessed must have been a hundred years old. The only artificial light in the room came from a pendant lamp that hung over the commissioner's desk, making him eerily hard to see. The seats of the chairs the two visitors sat on were set about an inch less above the floor than the normal distance of eighteen inches. The commissioner seemed to tower above them. He had contrived a cunning way to gain a slight psychological advantage over anyone who sat on them. He wasn't at all happy that Andrew had talked his secretary into granting him an appointment.

"How come *you* are here, Superintendent? I thought it was with Sergeant Vitkus alone. Personal, my secretary said. By the way, Vitkus, from what I've read about you in the reports and from the Superintendent, you're going a great job. He wants you to move up the ladder. Why don't you tell me why you should become a lieutenant?" The super started to answer for Andrew, but the commissioner brushed him off. "So, Sergeant, tell me. Go ahead, tell me."

"Well, sir, I'll tell you and it's not going to be what you want to hear..."

"What? What do you mean?" The commissioner leaned forward, his attitude had changed.

"Sir, I am a killer. I—"

"In the service? The army?"

"No, sir. In civilian life. I killed John Mohegan nine years ago. I—"

"Who? What?" The superintendent interrupted to explain about the unsolved murder in Southie in September 1941. "*My god*, boy! Why did you wait so long?"

"I..."

"Why didn't you let people know earlier? You lied and lied all along, didn't you?" He was demanding now. His large body leaning forward, a stubby right index finger, suddenly hostile, seeming to be thrown at Andrew with each threatening utterance. Andrew was not given the chance to tell the complete story. "*Oh my god!* Dammit! Don't you realize what this means to me, to the department? Cop admits to being a murderer! The mayor will be out of his mind! Darlene! Darlene!" He was calling his secretary. "Darlene, get the mayor on the phone right away. Right now! Tell him I have to talk to him. I have to meet him right away! *Oh my god!* Superintendent, you and me…You and I, we have to go meet with the mayor right away. Sergeant…Mr. Vitkus, we'll let you know. We'll talk to you later. Who knows about this? Who else knows? Never mind. We'll deal with you later. Superintendent! Were there any witnesses? There were? One? We'll find him wherever he is…" And then they were gone.

Darlene walked in. "He's a crazy bastard. I hate working for him. I don't know what happened, Sergeant, but I know he's mad as hell at you, and me too, for arranging the meeting. But they've forgotten about you for now. So why don't you get outta here 'while the going is good,' as John Wayne would say. Anyway, Andrew, I know you did something bad, I guess. I hope not. But they didn't do nothing to you yet. So get outta here! Go!"

Andrew, who until Darlene's imperative, was going to wait for the two men to return, stepped out into the noon sunshine. Darlene was right, he was still a cop until the mayor and the commissioner figured out what to do to him or with him. And he had to find a way to call Marie to give her an update. All of a sudden, he was hungry. He spotted a pizza shop across the street and down a few hundred feet. Maybe there's a phone there. He headed toward it, crossing the street. A '38 Buick was parked at a hydrant, its motor running and its driver's side window open. A young man, maybe Andrew's age, had his arm dangling with a lighted cigarette between his fingers.

The beat cop in Andrew took over. "Hey, buddy! I don't want to bother you guys…"—he noticed there was a passenger—"but the beat cop will be coming by and you're sure to get a ticket."

"Don't worry, pal. We're just gonna be here a few minutes. We've got some business in that bank over there. Here comes our guy now."

The third man grabbed the back door handle but had trouble opening the door. The driver turned to give him instructions. Andrew spotted the big .45 in his waistband. Andrew had no weapon, no way of warning anyone in the bank that they were going to be robbed except to get there before the robbers.

"Thanks, pal!" he said to the driver as calmly as he could. "Don't say I didn't warn you." He walked the four hundred feet as inconspicuously as possible and pulled open the heavy glass doors. He frantically looked for someone to alert that their bank was about to be robbed. He instinctively knew no one would believe him at first. He would have to lean across the counter and yell at the guy at the desk who would also instinctively think Andrew himself was a bank robber or a screwball. Instead, he yelled at the top of his lungs in the middle of the floor. "Listen, everyone! I'm a cop! This bank is about to be robbed! Call the cops! Call the station!"

There were customers at each of the three teller's stations. One old lady fainted and slowly fell to the floor. All the other customers and employees started to scream or cry. No one remembered how to call the police. The bank manager hit the silent alarm, hoping it would work this time.

Suddenly, they burst in behind Andrew. Two of them wearing handkerchief masks, waving handguns, and firing shots into the ceiling, screaming at the top of their lungs. The first one vaulted over the counter. He grabbed the guy he thought must be the manager. The second robber just screamed and hollered profanities, telling tellers to empty their cash drawers or be shot. Andrew was unseen behind a large fluted column off to the side. The vaulter forced the terrified manager into the open vault. Andrew stood only a dozen feet behind the one facing the ashen-faced tellers, trying to decide what to do. He had no weapon. His mind raced. An image of a chokehold move he had been taught and practiced over and over in the South Pacific flashed into his mind. He had never used it against a Japanese soldier. He knew if the robber turned and saw him, he'd be shot. He slipped off his shoes without bending over. Then as silently and as swiftly as a hawk on a mouse, he was on his victim with the chokehold. As the man began to slump to the floor, Andrew plucked the big .45 from his limp right hand. It was heavier than he expected. He grabbed it with both hands and showed it to the other startled robber, the one who had leaped the counter and who now had come out of the vault with a sackful of loot. He had the terrified manager in a headlock with a revolver stuck in his temple.

"Where's Eric? Where's Eric?" the robber screamed. "I'm going to kill this guy if I don't see Eric. Where is he? He's my brother! He's my brother!"

Andrew answered him, "He's lying on the floor. He's not dead, pal, but he's hurting. Why don't you drop that gun?" Andrew's voice was a command. The vaulter eased the revolver away from the Managers temple without realizing it. "That poor guy has gotta go home tonight with his pants all soiled. His wife's gonna be mad at him, but he'd rather have that happen than not go home at all. He's got kids at home waiting for him! Now if you shoot him, I'm going to blow your head off with Eric's big gun here. I used one like this on some Japs a few years ago." Andrew had never fired a .45 in battle. "Now, you gonna drop it?"

"No! I—"

Andrew's shot hit the startled robber's right shoulder. His revolver clanked on the marble floor. He fell backward into a desk and then dropped on the floor, screaming in pain. A muted silence, broken only by sobs and weeping, descended quickly on the large room. Andrew's one shot sounded like a bomb. It echoed off the marble walls of the bank as it would through the minds of those terrified employees forever.

"Listen to me, ladies! Listen to me! I *am* a cop, off duty. There's one more outside, the driver. I've gotta get him before he figures out what happened and takes off. Watch this guy on the floor, all of you. Hit him with a paperweight or something if he tries to get up and make sure they send at least three ambulances!"

The bright sunshine blinded Andrew for a few seconds. Then he saw the Buick pulling away from the curb down the street. The driver sensed something had gone wrong inside the bank. Andrew ran to confront the car before it could pick up speed. He assumed the stance, feet spread apart. Two hands on the big gun. The Buick began to roll. It headed directly for him. Behind it, dozens of people were going about their business. A few were crossing the street to the pizza shop. Andrew squeezed the trigger. The bullet blasted the passenger's side windshield. The car slowed down and careened into a couple of parked cars before coming to a complete stop about fifty feet away from Andrew.

His heart was pounding. He ran to the car and pulled open the driver's side door. "Out!" he said. "Out and face down. I'm a police officer. You're under arrest!"

*****

Two hours earlier in the mayor's office, two of the three men were trying to assess this morning's bad news and its possible impact on them and their offices. The superintendent was excluded from the mayor's and the commissioner's frantic ranting about putting the best spin on Andrew's confession. The superintendent brought the mayor and the commissioner up to date on the facts of John Mohegan's death:

- *Fact 1.* On September 14, 1941, a man named John Mohegan, 59, in the company of his brother and son, had been shot dead outside Fenway Park.
- *Fact 2.* The shooting had apparently been random, caused by a young man who grabbed a police officer's weapon and had fired the presumably accidental fatal shot.
- *Fact 3.* The case had gone cold many years ago.
- Fact 4. It was not a high-profile case.
- *Fact 5.* The victim's family recently sought to reopen the case, which the commissioner agreed to do.
- *Fact 6.* New this morning, a member of this Boston Police Department, Sgt. Andrew Vitkus, for reasons yet unknown, had come out of nowhere to admit to the two highest-ranking members of the department that he was the killer of the aforementioned John Mohegan.

The mayor was unsettled by the news. He usually looked for someone to take the hit in situations like this one. He kept on repeating himself, "I can see the headlines now, 'Boston Hero Cop Says He's Guilty of Killing a Man Ten Years Ago.' And the stories would follow, 'Is This a Cover-Up That Is Now Being Exposed?' and 'What Else Has This Cop Been Hiding?'" No matter what, the mayor knew the news would be bad for his next campaign. He wanted to move quickly. "Let's put him on leave, without pay. Take his gun away. But let's not give the public his name right now. We've gotta be sure he's not off his rocker and is looking for publicity or early retirement or something. We gotta remember he's a war hero."

"Bring Dennis, the media guy, in here right away! Tell him the facts of the case quickly. We're gonna need a news release."

In ten minutes, he had a draft. "Yes sir, Mr. Mayor. How about this?"

Decade Old Murder May Be Solved

Mayor and Commissioner said this afternoon that they expect to announce the name of the police officer who has confessed to killing Mr. John Mohegan of South Boston outside of Fenway Park on Sunday, September 15, 1941. The disclosure of the police officer's name to the public waits clearance from the city solicitor and the district attorney who have just been appraised of the situation. The officer in question has been stripped of his badge and gun and, in all likelihood, will soon no longer be a member of the Boston Police Department. Criminal charges are being considered. There are no limitations on trying someone for this sort of crime.

"That okay?"

The mayor and commissioner were in agreement. The former yelled to the media guy on his way out with the story, "Get that in the late afternoon editions today. This afternoon!"

He looked at the commissioner and superintendent and pronounced satisfaction. "He sounds like a creep, that Vitkus. How could he lie his way onto the force like that? I'll bet half the stuff we're hearing about him is all lies and crap. I—"

"Mr. Mayor!"

"What do you want, Julia? Can't you see I'm busy with the Commissioner and the Superintendent—"

"I know, Mr. Mayor, but you have to hear this. Captain Mulroony from headquarters has been calling here looking for the Superintendent and the Commissioner. He says there's been an attempted bank robbery just outside headquarters. Three men just tried to rob the savings bank across the street. All of them were captured though…by a cop."

"That's nice, Julia. That's nice. It will be a great story tomorrow. But we've got business here. Superintendent, why don't you take the call?"

"But, sir, Mr. Mayor…"

"Yes, Julia?"

"The police officer's name is Sgt. Andrew Vitkus."

*****

Four hours after the shootings, the scene at the site of the robbery was more exciting than the best carnival. There were hundreds of spectators as well as the police, firemen, ambulances, and fire engines. People running every which way, reporters and photographers. Lights flashing blue, green, orange, and yellow. Bank employees were being questioned and interviewed. It was a mad house, a carnival. And in the center of it all stood an out-of-uniform Sgt. Andrew Vitkus with a .45 stuck awkwardly but prominently in his waistband. TV guys and reporters were running around, trying to get quotes from anyone who looked like they could speak English into a microphone.

In spite of the pandemonium surrounding him, Andrew was anxious to talk to Marie. The FBI was on the scene, questioning the exhausted bank employees. "He did it all," they said, pointing to

Andrew. "He saved us. I knew we would have been killed, except for him. That one! He says he's a cop. He captured all three of them. Oh Jesus! Oh God!"

Andrew had to give his story to the FBI. All around him there were screams of joy and astonishment. Shouts and noise everywhere. In the middle of the madness was Andrew trying to think of how he could get a message to Marie. Then he saw his chance, a TV reporter in the back of a van with a big phone up to her ear. "Miss, how does that thing work?"

"I'm plugged into an outlet in that office building. See the cord. You can use the phone for a minute, but I want an exclusive afterward!" She had to show Andrew how it worked. He dialed. Busy. Dialed. Busy. What was she doing? *Talking to Ellen*, he supposed. He handed the phone back to the TV reporter. "What about—?"

"Next time. I've got to get out of here!" he said out loud to no one in particular. Then in the milling crowd, he recognized a fellow sergeant. He only knew his first name. "Sergeant Frankie, I need a ride. Home to Southie. Whaddya say? Where's your cruiser?"

"On the street at the back of this building. C'mon, let's go! Sarge, what a day for you. You're going to get a big promotion!"

They pushed through the crowd, got to the cruiser, and took off with siren blaring and lights flashing. It was five thirty. Andrew wanted to get home before the six o'clock news. He wanted to tell Marie what happened before she saw it on TV. Or before the phone rang and people started to come by. They made it with 15 minutes to spare.

"Thanks, Frankie. I owe you a cold one."

"No, you don't, Sarge. I've got a story to tell my kids tonight. 'Kids, see that guy on TV! Sergeant Vitkus. I drove him home tonight.'"

*****

Andrew yanked open the kitchen door, startling Marie who was making supper while the kids watched TV.

"Andrew, I'm so mad at you! It's one of the most important days. We prayed about it this morning. You were supposed to call me. You should have let me know what happened. I've been on my knees all day. Ellen and I have been on the phone. I've been worrying about you. I'll bet you didn't tell them, did you? Why do you have that silly grin on your face?" It was five past six. The phone rang. "I'm not going to answer it. I'm so mad at you!" She began to cry. She tried to shrug off his embrace but somehow found she couldn't.

He whispered in her ear, "I think you'd better answer it. It's gonna ring all night."

She pulled away from him and grabbed the phone off the wall. "Hello? Daddy? What? *Oh my god!* What?" She began to feel faint. "Andrew, I…I think I'm going to faint." And then she did…into his arms.

"C'mon, wake up, baby! There you are. The cold water works." The phone was ringing again and it's not gonna stop. "Lucy! Go answer the door!"

"But, Daddy, you always told us—"

"Go answer the door! Oh, it's Bobby and Ellen!"

And so began an evening they would remember forever. Telephone calls (Bobby Mo finally had to become the official call taker). Visitors. Friends. Reporters. Madness. Just like the atmosphere earlier that afternoon, only more personal. As the night wore on, a boisterous crowd filled the little apartment. Everyone in Southie was there.

"Sarge, this call's for you. The superintendent."

"Hi, Superintendent. You'll have to talk up. There is a noisy crowd here."

"Andrew, I want to give you a heads up. The mayor's on his way over with the commissioner. Those three guys this morning. All bad. Two brothers, Eric and Andy Brown. The other guy, the driver, was their cousin. They were from the Midwest, here to get away from the heat out there. They killed a couple, an elderly couple, down in Peoria—or some place like that—in a bank robbery last week. Thank God you got them all! Andrew, one last thing. Don't tell anyone 'til they get there and make the announcement. You're gonna skip right over lieutenant! You're gonna be a captain, Andy! Congratulations, *Captain* Andrew Vitkus!"

The mayor and the commissioner came. The crowd became less raucous as they listened to His Honor bestow sainthood a.k.a. the rank of captain on Andrew. Then they cheered and cheered and toasted Andrew with beer bottles and cans raised high.

The commissioner pulled Andrew in close as he shook his hand on the way out. "Andrew, *that thing* this morning...There was a little story about it in the afternoon papers, couldn't be helped. The morning papers will have a correction, just a little piece. Of course, that'll be overshadowed by everything that happened this afternoon, won't it? Last time anyone's ever going to hear about that thing, I'll tell you. OK, pal? Captain Vitkus. See you in the morning or are you gonna take the day off? You'll need to, after all this."

At seven, the triplets had been unwillingly carted off by the Callahans with the promise of all kinds of goodies they wouldn't find at home. The crowd didn't break up until everyone had watched the news again on each of the three channels on the three TVs in the house. Then they all left. Bobby Mo and Ellen were the last to leave. "Hey, Sarge. I'm gonna call Manny soon as I get home. It's only nine out there. He'll be excited. So excited." Then the two men embraced tightly for a long time. Their wives stood silently as copious tears cascaded down their cheeks.

*****

Marie and Andrew slowly undressed for bed. He could hardly take off his outer clothes. She waited for him to climb in.

"Andrew, I know you're tired. I know you're exhausted. It's been the most exciting day of your life, I'll bet."

"Maybe. St. Vith was pretty wild."

"And then there was the first day I saw you." They both blushed.

"Maybe so, honey. But this day started out so unpromising and it ended just the opposite, didn't it?"

"I guess it did. Andrew, do you remember what happened when you were dressing this morning? I asked you why you were wearing civies and you told me so the Commissioner—"

"Couldn't take my badge and gun away. I remember, honey. I remember. And it worked out, didn't it?"

"And you expected to be fired right on the spot, didn't you? All this time, you held on to this secret and when you finally told Bobby Mo, he forgave you, didn't he?"

"Yes, dear. Are you making a point here? I'm so tired."

"Hang on, big guy. Getting back to this morning, I know it was a long time ago now, but something else happened, right? I wanted us to pray like Ellen and Bobby Mo do." She wondered why she added the Mo. She rarely did. "I wanted us to pray. You made me put something on to cover myself, didn't you?"

"Yeah, so I could concentrate. You are so gorgeous. I love you so much."

"I love you so much too. But, Andrew, think about what happened."

"What happened?"

"Andrew, I prayed and asked Jesus to make good things come out of the meeting. That somehow you wouldn't get fired, that you wouldn't go to prison, and that our whole family wouldn't be embarrassed by all this."

"Yeah, we did."

"And what else, Andrew? What else did we ask Jesus for?"

"I dunno. I can't remember, Marie. I'm so tired."

"Well, big guy, I'll jog your memory. You scoffed at me. You just laughed. But I prayed that good things would happen to you…to us. And I said, 'Lord, that Andrew might even get promoted out of all this.' Didn't I pray that? Didn't I ask Jesus to promote you somehow? Didn't I, *Captain* Andrew Vitkus?"

The End

EPILOGUE

YOU MIGHT WONDER HOW IT all turned out for Bobby Mo, Sarge, and Manny in the years that followed. The easiest way to find out is to take a trip to Sullivan's at Castle Island on a Saturday morning in mid-June.

But rather than drive there and spend precious time trying to find a parking space, why don't you just rent one of Wadda Memori's Bubble Ships for ten bucks an hour? Wadda has operated illegally and invisibly on Day Boulevard forever, it seems. Once on board, you'll notice the ship will take you anywhere your mood tells it to go. You float slightly above the heads of the thousands of people who are having a good time on a beautiful day on Castle Island and on the nearby beach. Don't worry, you won't bother them. They won't even notice you. When you get to Sullivan's, which only takes a few seconds, you can look for familiar faces.

Sarge is the first one you spot. He's there, right in the middle of the crowd, at a round table with attached benches. He's standing with one foot on the concrete pavement and the other on the bench. His hair is turning gray, especially at his temples. His eyes, you can tell by the way his head is always imperceptibly turning, are surveying the crowd and looking for signs of trouble.

Marie looks up from her conversation with Ellen, "Andrew, you watching the girls? Lucy, especially. I know the three of them are flirting with those toughs from the hill. I don't want them to forget what they have to do in a half an hour."

"I got 'em, honey. But they won't forget. They love Mr. O'Bee."

"Here you go, Sarge. Here's your frappe," says Bobby Mo, still limping from the wound that almost took him out.

"Sir, can I please ask you a question?" The query came from a middle-aged, portly fellow wearing a wide-brimmed hat and a Hawaiian shirt and carrying several boxes of fried clams and french fries. "Sir, I think I know who you are. You're Captain Andrew Vitkus, aren't you? The famous Captain Vitkus of the Boston Police Department?"

"Not famous, but yes."

"But, sir...Captain, I come here all the time and I always hear all of the people around you, your family and friends. They all call you 'Sarge.' I don't understand."

"It's a long story, sir. A very long story."

"Gee, Captain—I mean, Sarge. I'd love to hear it sometime... honestly!"

"I'm not a good storyteller. But my buddy, Bobby Mo right there, is a good teller of stories. Come back in an hour and he'll tell you. Won't you, Bobby?"

"Yeah, OK, Sarge. In an hour."

You've only got your Bubble Ship for an hour and Mr. Memori cautioned you that it will disappear suddenly on the dot of your hour no matter where you are. So try getting Sarge's attention. "A half hour!" you yell in his ear. "A half hour!"

"Hey, buddy! A half hour, not an hour!"

"Yes, sir. Sarge...Captain, I'll be back."

Now look! There they come, the three of them. Lucy in the lead, giggling. They won't tell their parents yet but they've got a date with the freckled red-haired boys for the movies tomorrow afternoon, *Casablanca* starring Humphrey Bogart! But first, there's O'Bee. Here he comes in that old 1939 Plymouth sedan. His car moves slowly through the congestion in the cul-de-sac at Sullivan's. No spaces are available. But look, there's one marked with two old wicker chairs! Blocked. For some important person, Mr. O'Brien, a retired Boston police officer.

"Mr. O'Bee! Mr. O'Bee!" The three skinny budding teenagers run toward the space and pull away the chairs. When the smiling old man emerges from his car, they envelop him with kisses and hugs. Of course, they knew that frappes, fried clams, and french fries are in the offing. They also knew that Mr. O'Bee will surreptitiously slip them each a ten-dollar bill. "Don't tell Sarge, you hear?"

"We hear! We hear! We hear!" they yell cacophonously as they lead their captive through the crowd to the end of the line at Sullivan's.

Suddenly, right behind you, Sarge stands up. He puts his hand to his ear. He's listening for a certain sound. There it is again. *Honk! Honk, honk, honk! HONK!* "Manny's here! Marie! Ellen! Kids! The Lopeses are here!

You can hardly keep up in the Bubble Ship as two tables in front of Sullivan's empty and everyone pushes through the crowd toward the parking lot.

"We'll be back in a minute, O'Bee!" yell the girls as they join the rush.

The big van with California plates has already disgorged beautiful Antoinette, little Yilda, and Fernan. They're busy hugging their Boston cousins. Now everyone stands back as Manny pushes the buttons and levers and several motorized hydraulic actions allow him to emerge to cheers and clapping. His black eyes squint in the bright sunshine. Soon he's hugging all the Boston kids and kissing Ellen and Marie. He high-fives Sarge then salutes him.

"Where's Bobby? Where's Bobby Mo?"

Ellen speaks up. "He's back there at a table. Sarge just promised some guy that Bobby would tell him the story of why he's called Sarge, not Captain."

Whoa! That's right. You realize suddenly that your time in the Bubble Ship is almost up so you move swiftly back to the table where Bobby and the portly gentleman are talking.

The stranger speaks first. "Say, where did everyone go? There was a mob here a minute ago."

"They went up to greet Manny Lopes and his family. He's in a motorized wheelchair. Lives in Southern Cal and runs a winery there with his family. Comes here every year about this time to renew acquaintances with Andrew and me."

"Andrew?"

"Sarge. Captain. Andrew. Andrew Vitkus."

"So the three of you…?"

"Are best friends. The best of friends. Friends for life."

"Well, if you don't mind my asking, how? The war?"

"The war, yes. We all met in the middle of September in 1944. The war wasn't over. It had eight months to go. And in—"

Poof!

"Hey buddy, whatcha doing? You're cutting the line."

"I am? Oh, I'm sorry! I just wanted a frappe."

"Yeah, buddy. But you gotta go to the end of the line. It moves fast here at Sullivan's."

"Oh, OK. So I go to—?"

"The *end*, Buddy. The *end*."

The End

ABOUT THE AUTHOR

John J. Carroll has a bachelor's degree in civil engineering from Northeastern University. He has been the director of public works in Lexington, Massachusetts, the commissioner of public works for the Commonwealth of Massachusetts, and, most recently, the town manager for Norwood, Massachusetts.

John had six children with his late wife Marilyn, and later married his present wife Penelope, who has eight children. They adopted four after that, so he has helped raise eighteen children in all. He lives with Penelope near Boston.

This is Mr. Carroll's first novel.

CPSIA information can be obtained
at www.ICGtesting.com
Printed in the USA
LVHW090432151020
668666LV00006BA/594

9 781645 314028